P9-DHN-189

French-fried twins . . .

Jessica turned as a woman's voice, chattering quickly in French, floated down the hallway toward them. It was Madame du Noir! Jessica felt her flesh beginning to crawl.

"Hang up!" she hissed to her sister, cutting off the connection herself just in case Elizabeth didn't pay attention. "Listen!"

"What?" Elizabeth glanced toward the hallway.

"Quiet!" Jessica's heart was racing. "Don't talk—just translate!"

"Umm, she's saying—'I was going to—'" Elizabeth paused. A ghastly look came over her face.

"What?" Jessica shouted in a whisper.

"She said, 'I was going to cook them for dinner,'" Elizabeth continued in a strangled voice. "And then—'" She gulped. "'Then I'll put them under glass.'"

"Under glass?" Jessica drew in her breath sharply. In her mind's eye she could see a huge window being pressed down against herself and her sister, forcing its way down, down, down, as they lay tied up in a bubbling pot. "Get me out of here!" she cried.

SWEET VALLEY TWINS

◇ SUPER EDITION ◇

The Twins Take Paris

◇

Written by
Jamie Suzanne

Created by
FRANCINE PASCAL

BANTAM BOOKS
NEW YORK · TORONTO · LONDON · SYDNEY · AUCKLAND

RL 4, 008-012

THE TWINS TAKE PARIS
A Bantam Book / February 1996

Sweet Valley High® and Sweet Valley Twins® are
registered trademarks of Francine Pascal.

Conceived by Francine Pascal

Produced by Daniel Weiss Associates, Inc.
33 West 17th Street
New York, NY 10011

Cover art by James Mathewuse

All rights reserved.
Copyright © 1996 by Francine Pascal.
Cover art copyright © 1996 by Daniel Weiss Associates, Inc.
No part of this book may be reproduced or transmitted
in any form or by any means, electronic or mechanical,
including photocopying, recording, or by any information
storage and retrieval system, without permission in
writing from the publisher.

For information address: Bantam Books

If you purchased this book without a cover, you should be aware
that this book is stolen property. It was reported as "unsold and
destroyed" to the publisher and neither the author nor the publisher
has received any payment for this "stripped book."

ISBN: 0-553-48390-0

Published simultaneously in the United States and Canada

Bantam Books are published by Bantam Books, a division of Bantam
Doubleday Dell Publishing Group, Inc. Its trademark, consisting of the
words "Bantam Books" and the portrayal of a rooster, is Registered in the
U.S. Patent and Trademark Office and in other countries. Marca
Registrada. Bantam Books, 1540 Broadway, New York, New York 10036.

PRINTED IN THE UNITED STATES OF AMERICA

OPM   0 9 8 7 6 5 4 3 2 1

To Ashley Rose DuVan

One

"What an incredibly stupid book," Jessica Wakefield said scornfully.

Her twin sister, Elizabeth, looked up from the map in front of her. The girls were sitting at the kitchen table before dinner. "Which book?" she asked.

"This French phrase book," Jessica said. "See what it's called? *Speak French Just as a Native Might Do.* That gives you an idea right there."

Elizabeth tried to hide a grin. The twins, sixthgraders at Sweet Valley Middle School, had won a trip to Paris for spring break through an exchange program called *Bonjour, Paris!* Their plane was due to leave tomorrow, and Elizabeth couldn't wait. She'd spent all morning brushing up on her French and planning great places to visit. "Come on, Jess," she said, folding up her map. "It can't be that bad."

"No?" Jessica challenged her. She flipped

through the book. "Here's something travelers use every day. 'Il n'est pas encore mort.' Know what it means?"

"Umm . . ." Elizabeth wrinkled her brow. "'Il n'est pas' would mean 'he isn't,' or something, and—"

Jessica interrupted. "It means 'He's not dead yet,'" she said, rolling her eyes. "Can't you just see it? We'll be crossing the street and some guy will get hit by a bus, and we'll save his life by running to a phone and yelling 'Il n'est pas encore mort' into it." She snorted. "*Real helpful*."

Elizabeth laughed. "There must be useful phrases in there somewhere," she said, reaching for the book.

"I kind of doubt it." Jessica sniffed.

"Don't be silly." Elizabeth tried to sound firm. "They wouldn't put out a book like this if it didn't tell travelers things they need to know." Opening the book to the middle, she read aloud the first phrase she saw. "Like 'Gloire immortelle de nos aïeux,'" she said, using her best French accent.

"What does *that* mean?" Jessica curled her lip.

Glory something, Elizabeth told herself. She shifted her gaze to the other side of the page. "'Hail to the never-dying ancestors of long ago,'" she read, wrinkling her brow.

"See?" Jessica demanded.

Elizabeth snapped the book shut. "I guess that is kind of lame."

"It might come in handy if we were watching an army parade or something," Jessica said helpfully.

"They could bang the drums and we could say 'Gloire immortelle whatever whatever.'"

"'De nos aïeux,'" Elizabeth finished absentmindedly, reaching for a guidebook called *Prepping for Paris.*

"Show-off," Jessica said. "How do you spell that last word, anyway?"

"Umm . . ." Elizabeth searched her memory. "A-ï-e-u-x," she spelled. "It means ancestors."

Jessica gave her a look. "That's not a word, that's a sneeze," she complained. "How in the world do you get to pronounce a-ï-e-u-x 'eye-you'?"

Elizabeth shrugged. "French is a funny language," she told her sister. "You know that. We've been studying it all year long in school."

"Oh, school," Jessica said with a dismissive wave of her hand.

Elizabeth chuckled to herself. The comment was typical of her sister. The twins looked just alike—each had long blond hair, greenish blue eyes, and a dimple in her left cheek. But on the inside, they were completely different. Jessica rarely took school very seriously. She preferred to spend her time in long discussions with her friends about fashion, soap operas, and boys.

Elizabeth was much more studious. Though she always made time for friends and family, she loved nothing better than curling up with a good book, and she was especially proud of the sixth-grade newspaper she edited, *The Sweet Valley Sixers.*

Despite their differences, though, the two girls were the best of friends.

Elizabeth smiled at her sister. "Yes, school," she told Jessica. "Don't blame me if you don't understand a single word when we're in Paris. Who wrote notes to Aaron Dallas during class instead of learning vocabulary words last week?"

Jessica snorted. "Writing notes to Aaron was much more fun."

"Still—" Elizabeth stopped. *Well, it probably was more fun,* she admitted to herself. But she didn't say it out loud.

"Anyway," Jessica went on, "the things we learn in French class aren't any better. 'The pen of my aunt is green,' " she recited in a singsong voice. " 'The pen of my aunt is blue.' 'The uncle of my aunt is purple.' I mean, give me a break!"

Elizabeth had to admit, Jessica had a point. She remembered the language tapes that she'd been listening to almost every night for the last six weeks. The first line of one tape had been 'Oh, my! I am late for luncheon with the queen!' She shook her head and glanced at Jessica. "What phrases do you think should be in these books instead?" she asked, curious.

"Oh, all kinds," Jessica said idly. "Useful ones. You know. 'Where do the cute guys hang out?' 'Which way to the mall?' That kind of thing."

Elizabeth felt her mouth curve into a smile. "Like 'Seen any good videos lately?' " she suggested.

"Hey, yeah!" Jessica said. She grabbed a piece of paper and wrote furiously. "And how about 'What do you mean, we have to *walk* there?' "

"Well, it *would* be kind of fun to know how to say that," Elizabeth agreed.

"You bet." Jessica frowned and began to count on her fingers. "Let's see—seven days in Paris. If I learned, like, three phrases a day, that would be more than twenty phrases altogether." She sat back and grinned. "A pretty good start for a phrase book, wouldn't you say?"

"You're actually going to find out how to translate these?" Elizabeth stared at her sister in surprise.

"Well, *someone* has to do it," Jessica retorted, scribbling as she spoke. "Think, Lizzie. There must be thousands of kids who visit Paris and want to know how to say really important things. Like . . . " She considered. "Like 'way cool.'"

Elizabeth nodded slowly. "Maybe you're right."

"Of course I'm right," Jessica said confidently. She held the paper up in the air. "I bet I could publish this. I bet I could become a millionaire. I bet—"

"A millionaire?"

Startled, Elizabeth turned to see her older brother, Steven, enter the room. "What are you planning, a bank robbery?" he asked, grabbing an apple from the bowl on the counter. "That's about the only way *you* could make a million dollars. Yuk yuk yuk!"

"My book would have insults, too," Jessica went on, talking to Elizabeth as though Steven weren't even there. "Things like 'My brother is a total wimp.'"

"Must be some other brother," Steven grumbled,

taking a huge bite from the apple. "What are you doing, anyway? I thought you were getting ready to take Paris."

"We are," Elizabeth showed him the guide-books. "Jessica's going to make her own phrase book, that's all."

"Filled with phrases that are really useful," Jessica added proudly.

"Really useful, huh?" Steven looked thoughtful. "You mean with lines like 'Where can we go to shoot some hoops?'" Steven was on the basketball team at Sweet Valley High School.

"Hey, yeah," Jessica said, her eyes dancing as she wrote.

"Not a bad idea," Steven admitted, taking two more quick bites. "I'm glad I thought of it."

"Steven Wakefield!" Jessica protested. "You did not either think of it. It was—"

"Oh, and here's one you'll need," Steven interrupted. "It's about food, so it's, like, really important. You know what they serve you over there, don't you?"

"What?" Jessica glowered at her brother.

"Weird gunk," Steven said happily. "Frogs' legs and chopped-up snails and gross stuff like that." Elizabeth felt her stomach do a flip. "And you know what's worse?" Steven dropped his voice to a whisper. "They cover everything with strange sauces so you don't even know what you're eating. So you better learn to say 'Does my dinner have any intestines in it?'"

"Steven!" Elizabeth exclaimed.

"Gross!" Jessica was writing quickly.

"And if the answer is yes," Steven continued, "then you should learn to say 'I think I'm about to throw up.'" He finished the apple and tossed the core into the compost bin. "I wonder why they haven't taught us how to say *that* in school."

"It does seem kind of basic," Jessica agreed, writing down the last few words. "Thanks, Steven. Got any more phrases for me?"

Steven tapped his finger to his chin, looking knowledgeable. "Well—"

"No, he doesn't!" Elizabeth broke in quickly. She didn't think she could stand another Steven phrase just now. *Maybe I should take along some good American food,* she told herself. *Do they have pizza in France?*

Or, more to the point—
She swallowed hard.
Do they have pizza without intestines in France?

"Just ignore him," Jessica advised her sister a few minutes later. Steven had gone off again, chewing on yet another apple and muttering vaguely about boiled octopus stomachs.

Elizabeth smiled weakly. "Yeah, OK. But it's not easy."

"I know. But hey," Jessica said, brightening. "This is going to be *such* a cool vacation. What's the name of the family we're going to be staying with? The Monte—Montecarlos?"

"Monteclaires," Elizabeth corrected her.

"Whatever," Jessica said airily. "They sound so

neat—a girl our age, and an older boy who's prob-ably pretty cool himself."

"How do you know he won't be just like Steven?" Elizabeth asked.

Jessica shrugged. "Think about it, Lizzie. There can't possibly be two Stevens in the world. At least, I hope not." Jessica frowned, feeling a sudden pang of worry. "What's the brother's name, anyway? It's not the French name for 'Steven,' is it?"

"'Steven' in French is 'Etienne,'" Elizabeth re-plied. "And I don't think he is called 'Etienne.' Let me see . . ." She wrinkled her nose. "Oh, right. 'Alain'—that's it."

"Alain Monteclaire," Jessica said happily, almost tasting the name as it rolled off her tongue. "Alain. Yes, that'll do just fine."

"We're glad you approve!" Elizabeth giggled.

"He'll drive a really cool car," Jessica decided. Red? Purple? She tried various colors in her imagi-nation. No—deep blue. Midnight blue, that sounds about right. "Just a little two-seater, of course. A convertible." She gazed dreamily out the window. "And one night he'll say to me, 'Zhessica, voulez-vous like to go for a ride in ze country wiss me in my really cool car?'"

"He'd be too old for you if he can drive already," Elizabeth pointed out.

"You're just jealous," Jessica said grandly. "But it's OK. I'm sure Alain will have plenty of cute friends. And they won't be named Etienne, either. So we'll drive around the countryside under the stars, and he'll turn to me and say, 'And now, what about some pizza à la pineapple?' and I'll say, 'Oh, Alain, what a great idea!' and—"

"Sounds fun, Jess," Elizabeth broke in, rolling her eyes. She picked up one of her guidebooks. "Listen to this about the Louvre."

"Who cares about some dusty old art museum?" Jessica replied. *Honestly, Elizabeth could be so boring sometimes!* "Maybe Alain could take me shopping, too. 'Voulez-vous like to come wiss me to ze mall and do le shopping?'"

"Do you really think you could fit all you want to buy into a little two-seater?" Elizabeth asked, smiling.

Hmm. Jessica had to stop and think about that for a moment. "Well, it wouldn't have to be an ordinary two-seater," she answered. "Maybe it could have, like, a really big trunk. Hey!" An idea had just occurred to her. "Maybe he drives a limo!"

"Who drives a limo?" Steven clumped back into the kitchen and dropped a thin package on the table in front of Jessica.

"No one you know," Jessica said frostily.

"No one *you* know, either," Elizabeth reminded Jessica.

"But someone I'm going to get to know very soon," Jessica added, fluttering her eyelashes at Steven. "What's this package, anyway?"

"It's for you," Steven explained. "And it came by *certified* mail! Just think—certified mail for the certifiably insane."

"Oh, shut up," Jessica told him. *When I become president, the first thing I will do is make it illegal to have a brother,* she thought as she glanced down at the package. "To Mrs. Jessic and Elziabeht Wakefeild," she read. "*Someone* can't spell."

"It's from France," Elizabeth pointed out, looking at the postmark. "You don't suppose——" She lifted her head and stared worriedly at her sister.

"Do you think it's from the Monteclaires?"

"Probably," Jessica said. "It's probably a photo of the *really cute older brother,*" she said loudly, staring hard at Steven. "Sheesh, I sure wish I had one." Grabbing the envelope, she tore it open.

"What if they say we can't come?" Elizabeth asked, biting her lip.

"Hey, no fair!" Steven burst out. "That means I have to put up with you during spring break. My life will be ruined!"

"Cut it out," Jessica commanded. *Elizabeth couldn't possibly be right—could she?* She pulled out a single piece of paper. "That's it?" Shaking the package, she peered inside. *Nothing else.*

"What does it say?" Elizabeth wanted to know.

Jessica unfolded the paper and stared hard at it. "My dere Jessic and Elziabeht," she read aloud, trying to pronounce "Elziabeht" as it was written. "We have news. Grand-mama is bacome sick. We must all too Nice to care of her——' Huh?" Jessica screwed up her forehead and studied that line again. "If their grandmother is sick, why are they saying that's so nice?" she demanded.

Elizabeth reached for the letter. "Nees,'" she said. "It's spelled n-i-c-e, but it's pronounced 'Nees.' It's a town in southern France."

"Well, why didn't they say so?" Jessica grumbled. *They have to go to Nice, I mean "Nees,"* Jessica thought. Slowly she nodded. *Yup, that makes more sense. But what does this have to do with—*

"Oh, Jess!" Elizabeth put down the letter and stared at her sister, twisting her hands. "They're not able to host us at all! They're leaving town!"

"No way!" Jessica grabbed for the letter again.

"'We can not keep you as our gests,'" she read aloud, clutching the paper close to her eyes. "Of all the nerve!"

"Well, if they have a sick grandmother—" Elizabeth began.

"Who cares about their sick grandmother?" Jessica retorted. "They're supposed to be taking care of us!" *Of all the unfair things that ever happened—* She stared down at the paper again. "But we have found place for you to stay wile we be gone.' Wonderful." She let the letter fall. "It's probably some disgusting sixth-floor apartment with spiders."

Steven seized the letter. "Anything to get you out of the house," he snapped. "'Madame du Noir is a kind window woman,'" he read.

"Window woman?" Jessica repeated, scratching her head. "How can you be a window woman?"

"They mean she works in a glass factory," Steven explained importantly.

"No, she doesn't." Elizabeth gave Steven a little shove. "The Monteclaires just don't write English very well. They mean a widow woman."

Widow woman! That made more sense. "Sure,"

Jessica said thoughtfully, spelling the words in her mind. "Window—widow."

"Does that say she's a 'lovely' person or a 'lonely' person?" Steven asked Elizabeth, pointing to a line on the paper.

"Lonely, I bet," Jessica said sourly. She wrinkled her nose and slumped across the table, knocking her list of phrases for her book onto the floor. "Some wonderful trip this is going to be. No cool car. No cute older brother. I bet she won't even let us go shopping. We'll get to spend our whole vacation listening to some lonely old woman babbling in a language we don't even understand."

Elizabeth grinned weakly. "Oh, come on, it won't be so bad," she protested. "We don't really know—"

"You're right!" Jessica exclaimed. "It won't be so bad. It'll be even worse! She'll probably have a hearing aid that she won't ever bother to turn on, and we'll have to go around yelling at her in French at the top of our lungs, like this." She took a deep breath. "MADAME DU NOIR, THE TERMITES ARE EATING YOUR BATHROOM SINK!" Jessica groaned loudly. "I wonder how you say *that* in French."

Steven chuckled softly, still reading the letter. "Hey, listen to this! 'Madame du Noir a fiend to little childs,'" he read aloud. "Fiend! I love it."

"*Friend,*" Elizabeth said heavily, looking over his shoulder. "She's a *friend* to little children."

"If that's 'friend,' then where's the 'r'?" Steven challenged her.

Elizabeth started to say something, but Jessica broke in. "Great," she snarled. "Just great." *I know that letter is full of mistakes*, she told herself gloomily. *I know Madame du Noir isn't really a fiend, and I know the Monteclaires told us she was a lovely woman, not a lonely woman. And her house is probably perfectly nice, and she won't serve us lemonade à la toad, but still—*

The truth was, there would be no gorgeous Alain Monteclaire driving her around in his convertible. And somehow Jessica couldn't quite get the image of a fiendish old woman out of her head.

"Cooped up in some old house with bats and a fiendish old lady." Jessica closed her eyes and turned to the wall. "We might just as well stay home."

She waited for Elizabeth to contradict her. Sensible, solid old Elizabeth—

But to make things even worse, Elizabeth just rested her face in her hand and sighed.

Two

"Do you have everything you need?" Mrs. Wakefield asked anxiously.

"Oh, Mom," Jessica grumbled. The girls were at the airport, waiting to board their plane for France. "That's only, what, the fifth time you've asked?"

"Eighth," Steven said promptly.

Mrs. Wakefield smiled. "Sorry. I know I don't have to worry about a thing. You'll be just fine." Then she frowned. "But did you remember—?"

"Alice," Mr. Wakefield said sternly. "The girls are responsible. You need to relax and let them have a good time."

"Thanks, Dad," Jessica whispered. She squeezed his hand.

"No problem." Mr. Wakefield grinned back. "I remember how it was with my own mother. You'll be just fine." Then his face darkened. "Oh, by the way, do you still have the French francs I gave you this morning?"

"Dad!" Jessica and Elizabeth groaned together.

Their father looked sheepish. "Sorry."

Jessica squeezed her father's hand once more. She wasn't about to admit it, but she *was* a little worried—only not about French francs. Even after a good night's sleep, the thought of being cooped up with an old widow didn't exactly thrill her.

"Did you bring anything to do on the plane?" Mrs. Wakefield asked.

Jessica sighed loudly and gritted her teeth. "Yes, Mom."

"You can borrow some of my guidebooks if you want," Elizabeth said, rummaging through her carry-on flight bag.

"No, thank you," Jessica said in a brittle voice. "Why would I want guidebooks? It's just going to be one boring, dusty museum after another, that's all. And we'll have to help Madame du Noir up the steps in her wheelchair."

"Hey, it'll be like pumping iron!" Steven said happily.

Jessica glared at her brother. *I'm not going to enjoy this trip very much,* she thought. *But there's one thing I'm going to enjoy, all right—*

Getting away from Steven!

"Now boarding rows twenty-five to forty-eight," a voice boomed over the loudspeaker.

"That's us." Elizabeth stood up from her seat. Her throat felt suddenly dry. "Well—bye, guys," she said, pasting a smile on her face and picking up her flight bag.

Mrs. Wakefield took a deep breath. "Have fun!" she said brightly, reaching out to hug her daughters.

"And don't get into trouble," Mr. Wakefield told them with a grin.

Jessica rolled her eyes. "What kind of trouble are you expecting us to get into?" she asked.

Elizabeth laughed. "Really, Dad. I mean, Madame du Noir will meet us at the airport, and we have her phone number, just in case. What could go wrong?"

"But do you still have the French francs I—" Mr. Wakefield began. He stopped and grinned nervously. "Just kidding."

"We'd better get on the plane," Jessica said, picking up her own flight bag.

"One minute!" Steven bounced forward and grabbed Elizabeth by the neck. "Oo la la!" He giggled hysterically, kissing her on both cheeks. "Oo la la!"

"Knock it off, Steven," Elizabeth told him with a grimace.

"But zis is ze way ze French say good-bye!" Steven insisted in a silly voice. He made a move toward Jessica.

"Come closer and you die," Jessica threatened, balling one hand into a fist.

Steven shrugged. "Now if ze plane crashes, you must hold your nose like so before you plunge into ze icy water, no?" He grabbed his own nose to demonstrate.

"That's enough, Steven," Mrs. Wakefield said quietly.

"You can say that again," Elizabeth agreed. Meeting Madame du Noir was going to be stressful enough. The last thing she needed was to worry about plane crashes, too.

"Last call for rows twenty-five to forty-eight," the loudspeaker boomed.

"We'd better go," Elizabeth said, feeling nervous but excited at the same time. She gave her parents a quick kiss, hefted her bag, and headed for the gate, with Jessica following her. She was almost there when she heard her father's voice, echoing frantically through the halls of the airport.

"Elizabeth! Jessica!"

A little exasperated, Elizabeth turned back. "What is it, Dad?" she called. *What now?*

Mr. Wakefield came running over. "Here," he said, grinning weakly. He held out a small envelope. "We forgot to give you your tickets!"

"Can I get you anything to drink?"

Jessica looked up to see a flight attendant smiling at her. "Some iced tea would be great," she said. "Thanks!"

"Coming right up," the flight attendant told her. The woman leaned over to the row behind Jessica and spoke to someone in French. Jessica strained to hear. "Deux Seven-Up," she could hear a voice reply. *Two Seven-Ups*, Jessica translated to herself, grinning.

"I'm Katharine," the flight attendant told Jessica a moment later, handing her a plastic cup of iced tea. "Enjoying your flight?"

"So far," Jessica said. She glanced at her sister, who was deeply engrossed in some boring old book. "We're traveling alone. We're spending spring break in Paris."

"Awesome!" Katharine said. "I bet you'll have a blast."

Jessica smiled and took a sip of tea. Katharine seemed like a really nice person. Then a thought struck her. "Hey!" she said, burrowing in her bag. "Are you one of those people who can, you know, speak two languages?"

"Bilingual?" Katharine asked with a smile. "That's right."

Jessica pulled out the first page of her phrase book triumphantly. "If you have a minute, would you be able to help me with this?" she asked. "I want to learn how to say some really useful things in French. Like, how do you say 'He's totally gorgeous'?"

Katharine laughed and looked at the list on Jessica's tray. "What a great project!" she said. "Let's see. 'Gorgeous' would be 'beau,' so—something like 'Il est vachement beau' ought to do just fine."

"*Vachement beau*— Thanks a lot!" Jessica said, writing furiously.

"*Christine strained her eyes in the darkness,*" Elizabeth read, a tingle creeping up her spine. One thing about Amanda Howard's mysteries: they were never boring! "*Who's there?' she cried, wishing they'd remembered to fill the gas tank that morning.*" Elizabeth turned the page, her fingers trembling. "*A little old lady stepped out of the shadows, her teeth a beautiful shiny white and her black dress glistening in—"*

"Listen to this, Lizzie!" To Elizabeth, Jessica's voice seemed to boom like a gunshot. Wincing, she tore her eyes away from the story. "I just had the greatest conversation with the flight attendant! Know how to say 'This music is dorky' in French?"

Annoyed, Elizabeth wrinkled her nose. *Just when I was getting to the really good part in my book,* she thought. "Can you wait about twenty minutes?" she asked. "Christine Davenport's car has broken down on a lonely road, and I really want to see what's going to happen."

"Christine Davenport?" Jessica peered over the edge of the book Elizabeth was reading. "You mean that girl detective? Haven't you read all of them a gazillion times?"

"This one is brand-new," Elizabeth said. "Really, Jess. I'd love to hear your translations, but I'm right in the middle of this chapter. There's a little old lady walking down the road and—"

"Watch out for that little old lady," Jessica said darkly. "In books like that, little old ladies are never what they seem to be."

Elizabeth made a harrumphing sound deep in her throat and settled back into her pillows. "Well, I'll talk to you in about twenty minutes," she said, searching the page for her place. *Ah. —glistening in the pale moonlight,"* she read.

Good.

The shivers were back.

*   *   *

On her way back to the galley, Katharine stopped and squatted down by the edge of Jessica's seat. "I was thinking about your vacation," she said, opening a can of apple juice and offering Jessica the first sip. "Where will you be staying when you get there? With friends?"

Jessica made a face. "Well, it's kind of complicated," she said. "We were going to stay with this really neat family, but they had to leave town—so we're staying with some dippy old woman instead."

Katharine frowned. "Dippy in what way?"

"Oh, I don't know." Jessica shrugged. "It's not like I've met her yet or anything. But somehow I just don't get the idea that she's a very nice person." With a pang of guilt, she wondered if she was being totally fair to Madame du Noir. She strained to visualize her new hostess. Maybe Madame du Noir was beautiful and smiled a lot. But, it was hard thinking of her as anything except—

Jessica squeezed her eyes shut. *Except a witch,* she thought with a little thrill of fear. *She looks exactly like the witch in Hansel and Gretel.*

"Hmm." Katharine leaned forward thoughtfully.

"No offense or anything, but has the agency that sent you checked this woman out?"

Jessica scratched her head. "I don't know," she answered honestly. "I guess so. Probably. I mean, they wouldn't send us off to live with an ax murderer, would they?" She laughed to show how silly the thought was.

Katharine nodded slowly. Wrinkling her nose, she looked off into the distance. "You know, you and your sister remind me a lot of a girl who was on one of my flights—oh, around Christmastime."

"Mademoiselle!" A voice echoed from the row behind Jessica. "S'il vous plait!"

"Pardon, pardon!" Katharine said hastily in French, turning away from Jessica. Jessica leaned back in her seat. *Of course Madame du Noir isn't a witch,* she reassured herself. *There are no such things as witches. And anyway—*

Jessica's mind flashed back to the letter that the Monteclaires had written. "Madame du Noir is the woman witch has the most butiful garden in Paris," Mrs. Monteclaire had written. *Probably just a word confusion,* Jessica told herself. *"Witch" for "which." I remember when I used to mix them up myself—and English is my native language!* She tried to laugh. Just a word confusion, that's all.

Jessica moved uneasily in her seat. Katharine's words echoed in her mind. *Has the agency checked this woman out?*

She only wished she could be sure.

* * *

"'Is that right, my dear?'

Christine's heart sank as she realized the little old woman was speaking to her. 'You'll never get away with this,' she said, her mind searching desperately for some way to escape."

Elizabeth bit her lip. *Come on, Christine!* she wanted to shout.

"Christine gasped. The woman's teeth were growing longer and sharper before Christine's own eyes! At the same time, the woman raised her long bony fingers. But *now they looked far more like animal claws than actual human hands—"*

Elizabeth wished she could stop reading. But she couldn't. She read on as the little old woman changed into a horrible monster, a monster intent on tearing Christine into shreds and then wolfing her down in big mouthfuls. When she finally finished the book, Elizabeth forgot all about her promise to Jessica. She leaned back on the pillows and shut her eyes.

I'm glad I'm not Christine, she thought. *Her life is too—well, too adventurous for me.*

Elizabeth tried to take a nap. But something was keeping her awake. Something she was trying to remember. Something—important.

Elizabeth sighed and squeezed her eyes shut tight. *A letter,* she thought suddenly, and it all came back in a rush.

A line in the letter the Monteclaires had sent them. She could see it on the paper just as clearly as if the paper were in front of her.

"Madame du Noir are a woman who licks children vary much."

Licks—likes. Elizabeth knew it was only a translation mistake. She tried hard not to think of the little old woman attacking Christine Davenport. Yes. She swallowed hard. It was only a translation mistake— *Wasn't it?*

Three

◇

"We must be almost there by now," Jessica said hopefully. They'd been in the air for what seemed like days. Dinner had come and gone, and night had fallen outside. Jessica gently rubbed her legs; she had cramps from sitting in one position for too long. She raised the flap on the window and peered out. "Still dark."

"I think we've got a long way to go yet," Elizabeth said, stretching. "Don't forget, we're going close to halfway around the world."

"Well, somebody should invent a way to do it faster," Jessica said. "A rocket ship or something." *Maybe a rocket that goes through the center of the earth,* she thought to herself, nodding with approval. *Yeah. That would take, what, forty-five minutes?* "Forget this twelve-hour stuff."

Elizabeth smiled sleepily. "Traveling's a lot faster than it used to be. Remember, it used to take six weeks just to cross the Atlantic Ocean by ship." She rubbed her eyes. "And getting to California would take weeks more. You could never go to France just for spring break."

"Yeah, but that was back then," Jessica said. "They should make it faster *now*."

Elizabeth yawned. "Well, I'm zonked. I think I'm going to get some sleep. Night, Jess." She settled back into her pillow.

Jessica considered what to do. *I should look at some of Lizzie's guidebooks,* she thought. Then she shook her head. *Too much work. Also, kind of boring. Cards?* She wondered if she should get out the deck she'd brought along in her flight bag. *Nah. Solitaire's not much fun, and anyway there really isn't room to spread out the cards.*

As Jessica considered her options, Katharine stopped by, handing out pillows and blankets to passengers. "Having a blast?" she greeted Jessica. "Or should I say, 'T'amuses-toi bien?'"

"Umm, not really," Jessica answered honestly. "There's a pile of magazines up by the attendant station," Katharine told her, pointing toward the front of the cabin. "Why don't you go help yourself? Just don't forget the emergency procedures while you're out of your seat."

"Thanks," Jessica replied, unbuckling her safety belt and standing up. It was a good excuse to get some exercise, anyway. "I think I will."

"Red—rouge," Elizabeth said drowsily. To help go to sleep, she was going through the colors in

French. "Green—vert. White—umm, blanc. Black—"

She curled up into a tighter ball. *How do you say 'black'?* she wondered. For some reason, she couldn't quite think of the word.

Well, it doesn't matter, she thought. She continued with her list. "Yellow—jaune. Blue—bleu. Black—"

There it was again.

It doesn't matter! she grumbled to herself, trying not to think of Christine Davenport's little old lady—or the old woman who "licked" little children.

But she had a sneaking feeling that the French word for "black" *did* matter.

"What a stupid pile of magazines," Jessica muttered under her breath.

She stood at the front of the cabin, sorting through the selection on board the airplane. Either other people already had all the good ones, or else the airline was trying to bore all its passengers to death. *The Antique Lampshade Collector?* Jessica grumbled, dropping that magazine back into the box. "Give me a break!"

The others were no better. *Classical Music Illustrated* boasted full-color photographs of old Hungarian trombones. *"Exclusive! In this issue!"*

"Whoop-de-do," Jessica said, circling her forefinger above her head before throwing *Classical Music Illustrated* back into the box. *Tax Shelter Digest* didn't seem worth a second look. Neither did *Popular Hairstyles for Poodles.*

Jessica wrinkled her nose. *Where are the French fashion magazines anyway?* She tossed aside *From*

Wimp to Hunk Quarterly, reminding herself to buy Steven a copy for his birthday, and examined the last magazine on the pile. *"International Traveler,"* Jessica read. The cover showed a glamorous woman in a fancy coat glaring into the camera. *Sounds good,* Jessica thought.

Returning to her seat, she began to leaf idly through the pages. *International Traveler* certainly seemed to have a lot of ads, she noticed, mostly for perfume, jewelry, and fancy hotel rooms. Jessica found herself wishing she were staying at the Chateau de la Magnifique, which was advertised as being "right on the Left Bank." *I don't know what a left bank is,* Jessica thought, *but the rooms look pretty gorgeous.*

She flipped a few pages. There were too many articles about old pieces of art, and not enough about swimsuit styles. *Hey, an article on Johnny Buck's lead drummer,* she thought suddenly, leaning forward to check out the picture. *What a dreamboat!* Jessica wondered how to translate "dreamboat" into French. She stole a look at her sister, but Elizabeth was sound asleep. *Well, I'll just have to do it myself.*

"Let's see," Jessica muttered, "'dream' is, um—'rêve.' And 'boat'—" It was on the tip of her tongue—*ah, yes—* "Bateau.' 'Dreamboat' must be 'rêve-bateau.'" *Voilà, un rêve-bateau!* she thought, staring at the picture. *Who says I can't speak French?*

"Voilà, un rêve-bateau!" Jessica told Katharine proudly as the flight attendant passed by.

Katharine's eyes widened. "I beg your pardon?" she asked.

"Un rêve-bateau," Jessica repeated, showing Katharine the picture. "You know—a dreamboat."

Katharine frowned. "Oh, dear," she said slowly. "That would mean a boat that you would see in a dream—not a guy at all. You can't translate it literally. Why don't you try—let me see . . ." She thought for a moment. "*Le garçon est très beau.*' Très beau," she repeated, winking at Jessica and walking on.

Jessica bit her lip. She was a little embarrassed about her mistake, but after a moment she began to feel a little better. *After all, it's better than saying the wrong thing in front of a really cute guy—I mean, a "beau garçon"!*

Jessica flipped a few more pages. A picture sprang out at her—a photo of a girl who looked a lot like herself. Curious, Jessica caught the page before it could turn. The girl was about her own age. She was standing in front of the Eiffel Tower, a smile on her face. Jessica's eyes shifted over to the text beside the picture. It was headlined "Has Anyone Seen This Girl?"

"An American tourist," Jessica read slowly. "Visiting France"—blah blah blah—"was near the Bastille——" Jessica looked over at her sleeping sister. *What was the Bastille?* she wondered. *A castle, a neighborhood, a factory? Something important, anyway.* With a frown, Jessica returned to the text. "—in the company of an old lady."

Wait a minute. Jessica sat bolt upright. *An old lady?*

With a growing sense of uneasiness, Jessica read the rest of the article. Several blond American girls had disappeared over the past several months while visiting France. No trace of them had been found. When last seen, every one of them had been walking with an unidentified old lady.

Jessica's throat felt suddenly dry. The image of Madame du Noir popped back into her head—only this time, Madame du Noir seemed to have grown a few more warts on her nose, and her laugh had become even more of a witchlike cackle. Jessica chewed on her lip, wondering what to do. It was easy to imagine Madame du Noir leading these poor children through the Bastille (was it a dungeon? Yes, Jessica was almost sure it was a dungeon) and into a cage where she would fatten them up.

Jessica stared at the photo again. The girl in the picture did bear an uncanny resemblance to her and her sister.

She reached out to awaken Elizabeth. "Lizzie?" she whispered, tapping her sister on the shoulder. Elizabeth moved in her sleep and made a noise deep inside her throat. "Huh?" Jessica said, gently shaking her twin's arm. "Wake up, Elizabeth. I—" She swallowed hard. "I really need to talk to you."

There was no answer but the sound of Elizabeth's regular breathing.

"Elizabeth Wakefield!" Jessica said, raising her voice a little. "Please! I—"

"*Je ne suis pas encore morte,*" Elizabeth mumbled, not opening her eyes.

"Huh?" Jessica stared at her sister.

"*Je ne suis pas encore morte,*" Elizabeth repeated.

Then she tossed her head up against the window and started snoring loudly.

So much for that idea, Jessica thought. She drummed her fingers on the armrest. Once Elizabeth started talking in her sleep, she was almost impossible to wake up. She knew *that* from personal experience.

"Probably just as well," she said to herself. "What would Elizabeth tell me, anyway?" She knew the answer. *"Reality check, Jess!"* she could hear her sister's voice echo in her mind. *"Who says the events are all related? And besides—"*

"OK, OK," Jessica said aloud. She felt tired herself. Pulling a blanket up over her chest, she wondered vaguely what Elizabeth had said. "Je ne suis pas encore morte," she repeated. Somehow that expression seemed very familiar. *"Morte"*—that meant "death," or "dead," or something like that. She screwed up her eyes. *Je ne suis pas en—*

Of course! It all came back now. "It's that stupid phrase from *Speak French Just as a Native Might Do,"* she said, feeling silly for not remembering it earlier. *"He's not dead yet.'* I mean—" She strained to remember her French grammar. *"Je ne pas"*—"I am not." So *"Je ne suis pas encore morte"* means—

I am not dead yet.

Despite the warmth of the blanket, Jessica shivered. *What in the world could Elizabeth possibly mean by that?*

"Noir! Noir! Noir!"

The word echoed through Elizabeth's head. If

this was a dream—and she hoped it was!—it was one of the longest she'd ever had. Also one of the all-time worst. First there was the crazy old lady with long, sharp claws, who was trying to cut off her head. And now Elizabeth could feel the hard plastic of her chair at school, her French teacher and all her classmates screaming at her. "Noir' means black!" she tried to call out. "Black! I know my colors—I really do! Don't hurt me!"

"Noir! Noir!" The words were getting louder. Ricocheting like bullets, they pierced through her eardrums and sliced right into the center of her brain. Stifling a scream, Elizabeth pressed her hands firmly up against her ears. "Black is 'noir' in French," she cried desperately. But no one seemed to hear her.

Now her French teacher leaned over her desk. "How do you say 'black' in French?" she screeched while the other students kept chanting.

"Noir!" Elizabeth gasped for breath. "Noir!" Then suddenly her teacher's face was gone, replaced by a dark, lifeless shadow. "You can't kill me with noise!" Elizabeth tried to shout at the shadow.

Out of the darkness a new face appeared, an old woman's face she'd never seen before, a face that made Elizabeth shiver without knowing exactly why. The red lips seemed dark against the pale skin. Slowly the lips curved up into a smile, but it was a smile with no humor in it. In her dream Elizabeth gasped.

There was only one way out. *Wake up!* Elizabeth commanded herself, the words sticking in her throat. *Wake up!* It has to be a dream—it *has* to—it—

The posters on the wall of the classroom began to spin. *"Noir . . . noir . . ."* Gradually the voices withered and died. The faces became a sea of color. *"Rouge,"* Elizabeth whispered. *"And jaune. Vert. Bleu. And—"*

Before her eyes, the sea of color faded out. Suddenly there was nothing but a sea of black dots against a dazzlingly white background. *"Blanc,"* Elizabeth said, finding her voice at last. *"And—"*

She opened her eyes slowly. There she was, inside the airplane. There was Jessica, asleep in the next seat. A flight attendant walked slowly down the aisle. Elizabeth had never been so happy to be awake. Only—

She blinked.

The black dots hadn't quite disappeared yet. *"Blanc—and noir,"* she added in a whisper.

Jessica sat up and stretched as the plane touched the ground. France at last! And she'd finally had a pretty good sleep, too. If only she hadn't dreamed that stupid dream—what was it all about?

She thought back. There had been this old woman—a witch? Jessica shook her head. *Not a witch. Definitely not a witch.* She bit her lip. No, the woman had looked perfectly normal.

This perfectly normal woman had suddenly forced Jessica down a long corridor. Jessica remembered the woman's black-and-white polka-dotted scarf waving in the breeze as they walked together. As they walked to—

Jessica couldn't quite remember where.

"Did you sleep well, Jess?" Elizabeth asked.

"Umm, mostly," Jessica replied. "What did you dream about?"

Elizabeth frowned. "I'm not really sure," she said, "but I have this funny feeling I was dreaming about Madame du Noir."

"Really?" Jessica's heart started to thump a mile a minute. "So did I."

Elizabeth shot Jessica a look. "Was it—was it a nice dream?"

Jessica bit her lip. "I—I don't think so. What about yours?"

Elizabeth shook her head as the plane began to taxi to the terminal.

"Oh, well," Elizabeth said with a sigh, looking down. "Coincidence. That's all it is. Pure coincidence."

"Coincidence," Jessica echoed. Nodding, she began to gnaw at the edge of a fingernail. "Yup, coincidence."

Four

◇

"It's a very big airport," Jessica said in a very small voice.

"Uh-huh." Elizabeth felt a little uneasy herself. "All we have to do is follow those signs with a suitcase on them—see?" She pointed to the left. "That'll take us to the baggage claim—and that's where Madame du Noir is supposed to meet us."

A middle-aged man in a dark suit pushed his way between Elizabeth and Jessica without apologizing. Elizabeth clutched her flight bag tightly. "All these people seem to be in such a rush!" she told her sister, trying to sound calm and in control, as if she flew to France every week.

Jessica didn't answer. She moved closer to Elizabeth, her eyes darting nervously around the corridor.

"Turn right." Elizabeth followed another arrow. *Everyone seems to speak incredibly quickly around here!*

she thought, straining to overhear a bit of conversation. *That cute teenager over by the information booth—did he just say that he'd eaten three bicycles for breakfast?*

Well, probably not. Elizabeth wished she'd studied French a little more before leaving Sweet Valley. *Maybe if I'd played those language tapes on fast-forward—*

"Lizzie?" Jessica's voice broke into her thoughts.

"What is it?" Elizabeth could see the baggage carousels ahead.

"I was just . . . wondering." Jessica licked her lips. "What if we don't, you know, *like* Madame du Noir? What if she just isn't . . . our kind of person?" Elizabeth turned to face her sister. "What do you mean, Jess?"

"Well . . ." Jessica hesitated. "You know." Elizabeth thought she probably did know. "Are you talking about our dreams?" she asked. "Because dreams are only dreams, even if they're scary." In fact, Elizabeth discovered, she was having trouble remembering her dream. Now that it was daylight, the night seemed very far away. *Something about my French teacher yelling at me—and forgetting how to say 'black'—*It didn't seem all that important.

Jessica swallowed hard. "But—"

"We're just disappointed, that's all," Elizabeth said, heading toward the baggage carousel. "Both of us. We were really looking forward to spending spring break with the Monteclaires, and now that we have to spend it somewhere else—" She shrugged. "I think we just kind of overreacted. Look, there are our backpacks!"

"I don't think my dream was just an overreaction," Jessica said grumpily, hurrying to catch up with Elizabeth.

Elizabeth pulled her backpack off the carousel and hoisted it onto her back. "Well, I'll tell you, I'd much rather have Madame du Noir meet us right now than nobody at all." Shading her eyes, she glanced around the baggage claim for a person who might be Madame du Noir. A small shiver of fear started up her spine. *What if no one comes to pick us up?*

"Well, I hope you're right." Jessica picked up her backpack. "Come on. Let's go wait outside."

Paris is such a busy place, Jessica thought a few minutes later.

At least, the Paris airport is!

She leaned against a metal guard rail that blocked the way to the street. In front of her, a zillion taxicabs honked impatiently. Other cars roared up and down the road, swerving around parked taxis, pedestrians, and police officers. Every so often there would be the squeal of brakes, and one driver would lean out of his window and yell something at another driver in the fastest French Jessica had ever heard.

Good thing Elizabeth understands French, she thought, glad that her sister was beside her. *I can always count on her to translate.*

Jessica stared in front of her again. Across from her, a young man stepped off the curb. Jessica's eyes grew wide. He was walking straight into the path of an oncoming motorcycle! "Look out!" she cried in alarm, motioning to the man that he should go back. *How do you say "Look out" in French?* she wondered wildly. *Re—something.*

"Regardez!" Elizabeth screamed as the motorbike bore down on the man. "Regardez!"

The man looked up, a frown on his face. "Pardon?" he asked, hurrying forward.

"Le—le motorcycle!" Jessica screamed, jumping up and down.

VVVRROOOOM! Like a lightning bolt, the motorcycle zipped across two lanes of traffic, missing the man by six inches. There was a screech of tires rubbing against concrete. The motorcycle rider shook his fist at the young man. Then he roared away in a cloud of thick black smoke.

"Oh, man," Jessica groaned. Her stomach felt like it had just taken a ride on a Tilt-a-Whirl, and her heart was thumping so loudly Jessica was sure it could be heard back in Sweet Valley. "How did he miss?"

She watched the young man cross the street. He didn't look flustered at all.

The man jumped up onto the curb next to Jessica. "Do not worry, miss," he told her cheerfully, waving his hand in the air. "Everybody know that French dri-vairs are ze worst dri-vairs in ze world!"

"How long are we planning to wait here?" Jessica hissed in Elizabeth's ear a few minutes later.

"Until Madame du Noir picks us up, I guess." Elizabeth shrugged, trying not to look worried.

"Do you have a better idea?" *I wish we knew what Madame du Noir looks like,* she thought, scanning the crowd for someone who might possibly be an old window—that is, widow—woman.

Jessica shook her head. "Not exactly," she said. "I guess I was kind of wondering if we could go back inside the airport and buy pastries."

French pastries. Suddenly Elizabeth felt hungry. "We can't both go," she said thoughtfully. "But maybe you could go yourself and bring some back for me."

Jessica's face fell. "I don't think I could do it alone," she said softly. "The airport is so big, and everyone speaks so quickly—"

Elizabeth nodded, seeing her point. "OK," she said, grinning at her sister. "Maybe when Madame du Noir shows up." She looked to the left. *That woman over there? No, too young.*

Next to her, Jessica gasped.

"What's the matter?" Elizabeth asked, turning to her sister. "Duck!" Jessica commanded, pulling Elizabeth down to her knees behind the guard rail. "It's her! It's her!"

"What are you talking about?" Elizabeth's knee ached where it had hit the ground. With one hand she massaged it. With the other she tried to hoist herself back to her feet. "Honestly, Jess, I—"

"Shh! Shh! It's *her!*" Jessica whispered frantically.

"Madame du Noir?" Elizabeth tried to see over the top of the guard rail.

"Are you crazy?" Jessica grabbed Elizabeth's arm and pulled her back down.

"Ouch!" Elizabeth cried as her sore knee hit the ground again.

"She'll kill us both!" Jessica cried.

Elizabeth stared at her sister. "Would you mind telling me what this is all about?"

"It's the woman in my dream!" Jessica could hardly get the words out. She was shaking violently, as though she were terribly cold. "She led me down a dark corridor, and then she told me—"

"Your *dream*?" Elizabeth shook loose from Jessica's grasp and folded her arms across her chest. Nearby, a car door banged. "You knocked me down because of a dream?"

"It's Madame du Noir, I'm telling you!" Jessica looked like she was about to cry. "She's across the street, and she was in my dream—and it's not just that, Lizzie—"

"This is insane." Before Jessica could stop her, Elizabeth had raised her head to just above the level of the guard rail. "Where's this woman?"

"It's the woman in my dream, it really is!" Jessica grasped Elizabeth's wrist so hard Elizabeth was afraid she might cut off her circulation. "Don't you see her? She was over by the skycap stand."

By the skycap stand? Frowning, Elizabeth stared at the red-shirted men who carried luggage in and out of the airport for passengers. "I see a young woman over there, and a family with a couple of kids, and a man in a suit—" She sighed heavily. "Jessica, what *are* you talking about?"

"Look harder!" Jessica insisted, her voice quavering.

Elizabeth took a deep breath and let it all out with one puff. Then her eyes caught sight of an elderly woman wearing a black-and-white polka-dotted scarf. She was deep in conversation with one of the skycaps. "You mean the woman in the scarf?" Elizabeth asked. "It's probably not Madame du Noir at all. And if it is, she doesn't look danger-ous." Somewhere in the back of Elizabeth's mind, though, the face seemed oddly familiar.

"It isn't just the dream." Jessica was speaking softly, but there was an edge to her voice. "There was this magazine article—I read it last night on the plane—kids are disappearing, Lizzie! They're disappearing here in France! And the last time any-one sees them—" She paused for breath. "The last time they get seen, they're with an old woman. The same old woman I dreamed about, I bet, and I bet it's Madame du Noir, and I bet that's her over there!" Jessica was practically screeching.

"There must be hundreds of women in Paris who look like that," Elizabeth said slowly, patting her sister on the shoulder. "Maybe even thousands. And that probably isn't Madame du Noir at all." She couldn't remember the last time she had seen Jessica so hysterical.

Elizabeth looked down into Jessica's frightened eyes. She wished she understood exactly what her sister was talking about. *A magazine article . . . and an old lady who makes children disappear . . . and a dream . . .*

She caught her breath. "A dream," she muttered. "That's why she looks so familiar." In her mind's eye she suddenly saw it again. The dark shadow, slowly dissolving into a face that looked very much like the face of the woman talking to the skycap over there—

Elizabeth shook her head. *One old woman looks pretty much like another,* she thought. *Who says it's the person I dreamed about?*

"Ridiculous," she said at last. "One hundred percent ridiculous. I'm standing up, Jessica, and I'm walking over there, and I'm going to ask her if her name is Madame du Noir, and—"

"No!" Jessica clutched at her sister's hand. "You can't!"

A snatch of conversation floated over from the skycap stand. Elizabeth strained to catch it. "Something something searching," she heard the woman say, glad to have caught one word. Then the skycap asked a question, but she couldn't tell what. The old woman looked at a piece of paper and started to speak.

"Ay-lee-sa-bess and Zhes-see-ca Oo-ake-feel!" Elizabeth heard clearly.

"Come on. Let's go." Elizabeth stood up and settled her flight bag over one shoulder. "That's Madame du Noir. It's got to be."

Jessica bit her lip. "Don't do it, Lizzie, please," she begged. "Something's . . . wrong. I can—I can feel it in my bones."

Elizabeth rolled her eyes. "Are you planning to stay here all night, Jess?"

"You can't leave me!" Jessica clutched her twin's wrist even tighter than before. "I don't like that look in her eye, and I'm *telling* you, there was this magazine article about kids who look *just like us* and how they're disappearing, and—" She paused. "What's she saying now?"

"Umm . . ." Elizabeth wrinkled her forehead and leaned closer. "Something about the Bastille. I guess she lives near there, or something."

The Bastille! Jessica stared at her sister in horror. "That proves it!" she said, clenching her teeth. "That's the neighborhood where the other girl vanished—you know, the one in the magazine!"

"I don't even know what you're talking about!" Elizabeth protested.

"Well, I tried to wake you up to show you," Jessica said, feeling as if she were about to cry. "But I couldn't. You just kept babbling about how you weren't dead yet!"

Elizabeth turned pale. "I did what?" she asked.

"You kept saying it," Jessica told her. "You said it, like, eight times. In French. Je ne pas something or other."

"Je ne suis pas encore morte," Elizabeth said automatically. She bit her lip. "I really said that—in my dream?"

Jessica nodded slowly. *And I only wish this were a dream, too,* she thought miserably.

"This is totally crazy." Elizabeth spoke with determination. Before Jessica could stop her, she lifted her head all the way above the guard rail. Leaning out toward the skycap, she opened her mouth to speak—

And then a look of terror came over her face.

"What is it?" Jessica hissed.

"Oh, man." Elizabeth settled slowly back into their hiding place. "Oh—man."

"What is it?" Jessica asked urgently. "Tell me!"

Elizabeth licked her lips. "I think she said, 'Those girls—'" She swallowed hard. "'Those girls aren't ever going home again.'"

Jessica sat up, not even bothering to say "I told you so." "That's it," she said briskly, grabbing Elizabeth by the collar and slipping out toward the first taxicab in line. "We're out of here!"

"Those girls aren't ever going home again."

As the twins dashed toward the taxicab, everything Jessica had said was a jumble in Elizabeth's mind. Magazine articles? The Bastille? What did an old jail have to do with kids disappearing? And how much should she believe in dreams?

But one thing was for sure.

When someone says you aren't ever going home again—you run!

Opening the passenger door of the taxicab, Elizabeth stole a look at the old woman. At that very instant the woman looked up so Elizabeth could see her face.

Elizabeth shuddered. There was no doubt about it. The woman in her dream was the same person as the woman who was standing in front of her!

Madame du Noir—if it was Madame du Noir—stared down at a piece of paper in her hand. When she looked up again, she was smiling. "Ay-lee-sa-bess!" she called, waving to get Elizabeth's attention. "Zhes-see-ca!" *It's Madame du Noir, all right,* Elizabeth thought, wishing she'd never come to Paris at all.

Madame du Noir's black-and-white scarf danced in the breeze. Elizabeth gulped. All she could remember was the zillions of black and white dots that had ended her dream.

"Hurry!" she urged Jessica. Together they jumped into the cab. Elizabeth slammed down the door locks and turned to the driver.

"Centre Pompidou," she said quickly. It was the only place in Paris whose name she could remember. "And fast!" she added unnecessarily. The cab had already pulled out with an alarming screech.

"Did you see her horrible grin?" Jessica whispered.

"Definitely evil," Elizabeth said with a shiver. She settled back against the cab's seat cushions. "At least we've escaped."

"You think we've escaped?" Jessica asked, her eyes wide. "Think again!"

With a tingle of terror, Elizabeth turned to look. Behind them, a second cab was pulling into traffic. And next to the driver sat Madame du Noir.

"She's following us," Jessica groaned.

Elizabeth took a deep breath. "Do you speak English?" she asked the driver.

Turning around, the driver stared at Elizabeth quizzically. The cab lurched sickeningly to the left. "Pardon?" he said.

"Never mind!" Elizabeth clutched Jessica's arm. "I wonder how you say 'Lose that cab that's following us!' in French."

Jessica's lips were pale. "I'll make a note of it for my phrase book," she promised.

Five

It's not like I'm jealous or anything, Steven told himself with a sigh. It was the second morning of spring break, and he sat at the kitchen table, staring at a piece of paper in front of him.

PLANS FOR SPRING BREAK, the paper read. P. S. EAT YOUR HEARTS OUT ELIZABETH AND JESSICA!!!!

Beneath that was a list—a very short list. 1) PLAY VOL-LEYBALL AT THE BEACH, Steven had written. 2) GO ROLLER-BLADING. 3) SURF. Now Steven clicked his pen and wrote a little note in parentheses: CAN'T SURF IN PARIS. HA!

What else? Steven ran his hand through his hair and tried to think.

Clicking his pen off and then on again, he added a new line. "Number four," he muttered to himself. "Play *more* volleyball down at the beach."

"Planning your spring break?" Mr. Wakefield asked, coming into the kitchen. He poured himself a cup of tea.

"Sort of." Steven glowered at the paper.

Mr. Wakefield stirred in some sugar. "Hope you're not jealous of your sisters and their trip."

"Jealous? Are you out of your mind?" Steven narrowed his eyes and frowned at his father. "Who would want to go to France, anyway? Now if you wanted to send me someplace interesting . . ."

Mr. Wakefield smiled. "Glad to hear it," he told Steven, clapping him on the back and walking out into the living room.

Jealous. Yeah, right. Steven snorted. *Who said I was jealous?* He looked once more at the paper in front of him. "Number *five*," he grumbled, writing quickly. "Play even *more* volleyball. Down at the beach." He paused. "Bet they don't play beach volleyball in Paris."

Steven grimaced. *Well, maybe I'm a little bit jealous. All right, all right, maybe a little more than that, OK?*

The phone rang. "I'll get it!" Steven jumped up quickly, glad to get away from his list. He picked up the receiver. "Hello!" he sang out. "Wakefield residence!"

"Ah, Mees-tair Oo-ake-feel!" a voice said. Steven frowned. The voice seemed a million miles away. Static crackled through the wires. And what had the voice said? He thought about saying "I beg your pardon?" into the mouthpiece, but settled instead for "Huh?"

"Mees-tair Oo-ake-feel?" the voice continued, a little clearer this time. *A woman,* Steven thought. *Now why would a woman be calling me? Especially a woman with a weird accent.* He still couldn't quite tell what the voice was saying. "Umm, are you selling encyclopedias or something?" he began. "Because if you are—"

"Mees-tair Oo-ake-feel, you must come at once!" the voice went on, rising in pitch. Steven strained to hear the words through the buzzing noises. *Stupid phone company!* "Your daugh-tairs have runned away!"

Daugh-tairs? Steven held the receiver away from his ear and frowned at it. *What in the world are daughtairs? And how can they run away?* "Uh, ma'am—"

"Come at once, good sir, I beg it of you!" The voice sounded frantic.

All at once it hit Steven. What else? It had to be Joe Howell, his so-called best friend, playing stupid jokes over the phone. "Joe?" he barked into the receiver. "That you? Because if it is, I'm telling you, this is pretty darn lame."

"Lame?" The voice sounded offended. "I am not lame! All in town shall tell you, Madame du Noir walk quite well without e-ven a cane!"

Madame du Noir? Steven's stomach did a somersault. This wasn't Joe trying to be funny. This was the woman the twins were staying with, calling all the way from France. Not only that, she was having a cow over the phone—and she seemed to have mistaken him for his father! "Um—just a minute," he said. Covering the mouthpiece with his hand, he yelled into the living room. "Hey, Mom and Dad! Better come quick! Sounds like the twins are history!"

"What?" Mrs. Wakefield dashed into the kitchen

and snatched the phone out of Steven's hand. "Hello! . . . Yes?"

"Whatever happened to 'please' and 'thank you'?" Steven muttered under his breath, staring at where the phone had been a second ago. His father came into the kitchen and stood beside him, a worried look on his face.

"Gone?" Mrs. Wakefield was clutching the phone so tightly, Steven was almost afraid it would snap in two. "Are you sure? . . . At the airport?" Her face paled as she listened some more. "They took a taxicab to—to where?"

"Hey, cool," Steven said, grinning. "I didn't think they'd have the guts."

"Cut it out, Steven," his father said darkly.

Mrs. Wakefield's forehead was wrinkled with alarm. "Let me get this straight. My daugh-tairs—I mean, my daughters—took a cab to the Centre Pompidou and now they're missing? But how—" She covered her mouth with her hand. "Yes. Yes. Golden hair, yes. And eyes of blue— Yes, Madame du Noir, it sounds just like them—"

Steven couldn't remember the last time he'd seen his mother so upset. *Even when I went surfing during that thunderstorm,* he thought resentfully. *Even then she was calm compared to this!* He folded his arms. *I mean, not that I'm jealous or anything.*

"Yes, Madame, right away," Mrs. Wakefield went on in a brittle voice. "Where can we reach you?" She listened for a moment, wrote down a number, and then hung up the receiver with a bang.

"Pack your bags," she instructed the rest of her

family. "Just as soon as I call the police, we're heading for Paris!"

The airport was bad enough, Elizabeth thought,
looking around the Centre Pompidou. *But this is ridiculous!*

The Centre Pompidou was part shopping mall,
part museum, and part civic center. It was jammed
with people. Music pulsed through the crowd, and
from every direction Elizabeth heard French being
spoken far too fast for her to understand. Everyone
seemed to have a place to go and a reason for going
there. *Everyone but us, that is,* Elizabeth thought
wearily, wishing she could enjoy the exhibits instead
of trying to figure out a good hiding place.

For what seemed like the hundredth time, she
picked her backpack up off the floor and hooked it
over her shoulders. It really was way too heavy to
be dragging around Paris like this—but where else
could they leave their luggage?

"I don't know how much longer I can keep
walking," Jessica said. She leaned over and poked
her sister in the ribs. "Don't you think we've lost
her by now?"

"Probably." Elizabeth walked on a few paces. "I
mean, face it, we're kind of lost ourselves." She
gave a nervous little laugh. "This is one humongous place."

Jessica licked her lips. "You're telling me. Hey,
umm, there's a little coffee shop up there." She
pointed to the right. "Maybe we could get a little
bite to eat?"

"Well . . ." Elizabeth hesitated. "Shouldn't we decide what we're going to do first?" *It does smell awfully good. . . .*

"But I'm *really hungry*." Jessica opened her eyes very wide and put on her most pitiful face. Elizabeth couldn't help grinning. Jessica could be very convincing with that look.

"All right," she decided. "I'm kind of hungry myself. Should I order, or—"

Jessica nodded quickly. "I'll—I'll find us a table."

"OK." *My French is better than Jessica's, anyway,* Elizabeth thought as she made her way to the counter.

"Bonjour, bonjour!" A stocky dark-haired man looked down at her with a friendly smile. At least Elizabeth *thought* that was what he was saying. He was speaking so quickly, she couldn't be sure.

"Umm . . . bonjour, bonjour," she said, flashing him a shy smile. "Umm . . . deux croissants, please—I mean, s'il vous plait." Just in case her pronunciation wasn't quite right, she pointed firmly to the croissants inside the glass case.

The man grinned. Reaching for the croissants, he let fly a torrent of French.

"Umm . . . pardon?" Elizabeth asked cautiously.

The man grinned again and repeated it more slowly. This time Elizabeth picked out a few words. "Elephant . . . manger . . . poisson." *Elephant?* she thought, scratching her head. *Elephant, eat, and fish. Huh? Why would he be telling me about an elephant eating a fish?*

The man plunked two croissants down on the

counter. Elizabeth decided she must have looked totally confused, because he said it once more—incredibly slowly this time. *Almost as slowly as the language tapes,* she thought with a shake of her head. And now it all became clear. "Not 'elephant,'" she muttered, looking around for Jessica. "He said 'enfant'—'child.'" *And 'croissant.' 'Not 'poisson!'"*

"He didn't say 'Elephants eat fish,'" she said distractedly, setting the croissants on the table where Jessica waited. "He said 'My child likes to eat croissants, too.'"

"What are you talking about?" Jessica asked curiously.

"Never mind." *This whole country is so confusing,* Elizabeth thought. A nagging doubt was creeping into her head. "Listen, Jessica. I've been thinking about what Madame du Noir said back there at the airport."

"I will *never* forget it," Jessica said with a shudder. She took a bite of croissant. "She said 'Those girls aren't ever going home again.'"

Elizabeth unwrapped her own pastry. "But what if she didn't?"

Jessica stopped chewing. "What do you mean?"

"Well, I'm having trouble understanding what people are saying," Elizabeth admitted. "They all talk so fast—"

"So what?" Jessica swallowed.

"So maybe that's not what Madame du Noir said," Elizabeth suggested. "I know I definitely heard her say 'girls.'"

Jessica raised an eyebrow and took an even bigger bite.

"And she definitely said 'home,'" Elizabeth went on. "But maybe the whole thing wasn't 'Those girls aren't ever going home again.' Maybe it was . . ." She thought hard. "Maybe she really said, 'I'm taking those girls home with me.'"

Jessica snorted. "Some translator *you* would make!"

"Sorry," Elizabeth shrugged, embarrassed. "But the point is, maybe we ran too soon. Maybe we should have stayed and talked to her, found out what she was really like. I think—I think we should call her and apologize," she blurted out before she could change her mind. "I bet she's gone home by now."

To Elizabeth's surprise, Jessica nodded slowly. "Maybe you're right," she said after a moment. "Seeing Paris this way is kind of a bore. These backpacks are pretty heavy, you know. And my hair is a mess."

"Your hair?" Elizabeth repeated blankly. "What's that got to do with anything?"

Jessica looked at Elizabeth as though she had turned purple all over. "She'll have a shower and a place to plug in my blow dryer," she said in exasperation. "I mean, they have electricity in France, don't they?"

"Yes," Elizabeth replied, stifling a laugh.

"Then what are we waiting for?" Jessica stuffed the last of her croissant in her mouth and reached down for her backpack. "I also doubt that the *Bonjour, Paris!* people would let us stay with an ax murderer. Would they?"

Elizabeth laughed out loud this time as she

struggled to her feet. *Of course*, she thought, surprised at how sensible Jessica was sounding. *Why didn't I think of that?* "I guess you're right."

Jessica picked up her backpack. "I can't wait to get rid of this thing. You know what? Maybe I'll even take a bubble bath." She sighed dreamily.

Elizabeth smiled, starting to perk up a little. "That sounds nice." She took a deep breath. "It'll be embarrassing, but we'll just make that call and apologize. That's all there is to it."

Jessica looked pointedly at Elizabeth. "Of course, you'll have to do all the talking."

"Me?" Elizabeth frowned. "But—"

"I mean, let's face it," Jessica said virtuously. "I can't speak a *word* of French."

"It's ringing." Elizabeth said a few minutes later. The twins were at the pay phone near the Pompidou entrance. "I really don't like doing this, Jess. . . ."

"I know." Jessica patted her sister on the back. "You're a hero."

There was a sound outside the booth. A woman's voice, chattering quickly in French, floated down the hallway toward them. Jessica turned. It was Madame du Noir! Jessica's scary dream rushed back to her. She forgot all about her wish to drop off her bags and take a bath. Hearing Madame du Noir's voice, she felt her flesh beginning to crawl. "Hang up!" she hissed to her sister, cutting off the connection herself just in case Elizabeth didn't pay attention. "Listen!"

"What?" Elizabeth glanced toward the hallway.

"Quiet!" Jessica's heart was racing. "Don't talk—just translate!"

"Umm, she's saying, 'I was going to—'" Elizabeth paused. A ghastly look came over her face.

"What?" Jessica shouted in a whisper.

"She said, 'I was going to cook them for dinner,'" Elizabeth continued in a strangled voice. "'And then—'" She gulped. "Then I'll put them under glass.'"

"Under glass?" Jessica drew in her breath sharply. "Does she mean us?" But she was afraid she already knew the answer.

Elizabeth shivered. "I don't want to be put under glass," she said. "I—I already feel like . . ." She paused. "Like I can't breathe."

Jessica pressed her body against the door of the phone booth. In her mind's eye, she could see a huge window being pressed down against herself and her sister, forcing its way down, down, down, as they lie tied up in a bubbling pot. "Get me out of here," she mumbled, reaching for the door of the phone booth.

"Wait." Elizabeth clutched her sister's arm.

Jessica peered around the corner. Madame du Noir was with a security guard. And both of them were coming right toward the twins!

Jessica clutched Elizabeth as tightly as she could as the figures came nearer. She saw a piece of paper in Madame du Noir's hand. *A photograph of us,* she thought with dread. *She's out to get us for sure!* Madame du Noir's eyes seemed to glitter evilly in the dim light. Jessica tried to make herself as small and inconspicuous as possible.

The footsteps passed by. "Maybe—maybe I heard that wrong," Elizabeth said helplessly as Madame du Noir disappeared around the corner. "What does 'under glass' mean, anyway? Who says it's something terrible?"

Jessica looked meaningfully at her sister. "Under glass," she said slowly and deliberately. "Picture this. A huge pane of glass the size of a roof coming down on top of us and—"

Elizabeth bit her lip. "But maybe—"

"And pressing *hard*," Jessica added firmly.

Elizabeth shut her eyes. "And pressing hard," she repeated in a small, terrified voice.

Six

"Now what?" Elizabeth asked a few minutes later.

"We just keep on walking." Jessica squared her shoulders and set off down a side street near the Centre Pompidou. "Anything to get away from that place."

Elizabeth glanced over her shoulder at the building behind them. "I'm glad Madame du Noir didn't see us," she said. The old woman's words still tumbled through her head. "I was going to cook them for dinner. . . ." She shuddered. What had the words been in French? "Je . . ."

Funny. She couldn't remember.

They turned a corner. Elizabeth adjusted her backpack. "Don't you think maybe we should tell the police or something?" she asked.

Jessica scoffed. "And say what?"

"Well . . ." Elizabeth considered. "We'd say that

this crazy old woman is chasing us all over Paris. We'd say she told a skycap that we weren't ever going home, and then she told a guard at the Centre Pompidou that she'd cook us and put us under glass."

Jessica rolled her eyes. "Oh, I'm *sure* they'd believe that," she said. "Little old ladies in Paris probably go around putting children under glass all the *time*. I bet it's their biggest crime problem."

Elizabeth's shoulders slumped forward. The story did seem a little way-out. "I see what you mean."

"They'd never buy it," Jessica said with a shrug. "Even if we could speak French real well. Which we can't."

Elizabeth frowned. Madame du Noir's voice pulsed through her memory once again. "And then I'll put them *under glass*." *In French, it was—let me see . . .*

For the second time, Elizabeth drew a complete blank.

"Even worse," Jessica added, "they'd probably put us in a squad car and take us right to Madame du Noir's house. Door-to-door service. Then they'd pat us on the heads and say 'You will be pair-fectly safe here, dear girls,' and just as soon as they'd leave, Madame du Noir would plug in her trusty frying pan and *whomp*." She clutched her stomach. "We'd be meat."

"Literally," Elizabeth added dismally.

"Let's not think about it," Jessica said with a shiver. "It's too awful—" Suddenly she broke off and grabbed Elizabeth's arm. "Lizzie!" she hissed. "It's *her!*"

"What? Where?" Elizabeth looked around in terror. *I wonder if this is what it feels like to have a heart attack,* she thought. "Where?"

"Not really her." Jessica's eyes focused on a newsstand in front of them. "But look at the picture on the front page of that newspaper!"

Elizabeth followed Jessica's gaze. The black-and-white photo was somewhat grainy. It showed an old woman who looked vaguely familiar. Little prickles rose on the back of Elizabeth's neck as she bent to examine the photo more closely. "She does look like Madame du Noir," she said slowly. "But lots of women—"

"Her neck," Jessica whispered. "Look at what she's got on her neck."

Elizabeth took a step nearer. "Oh, man," she said softly. The woman in the picture was wearing a black-and-white polka-dotted scarf. "It looks just like the scarf that—" Her mouth felt suddenly dry.

Jessica broke in. "The scarf that Madame du Noir was wearing."

For a moment neither of the twins said a word. At last, Jessica cleared her throat. "What does it say, Lizzie?" She bit her lip and poked a finger at the text beside the picture.

"The police . . ." Elizabeth began. *What was that next word?* She shook her head. It wasn't familiar. "The police something something girls." *Yes, that was right.* The next word was familiar, too. "The police something something disappearing girls," she said proudly.

"What?" Jessica turned to Elizabeth and grabbed her shoulder. There was a wild expression on her face.

"I said—" Elizabeth was about to repeat herself, when the full meaning of the sentence hit her. "Oh, man," she said again. "Oh, man."

"What's the rest of it?" Jessica tightened her grip on Elizabeth's shoulder.

"Disappearing girls," Elizabeth repeated. "Then some more words I don't know, and it ends 'a woman who looks like this.'" She took a deep gulp of air and let it out slowly.

The police, she thought grimly. *Disappearing girls. And a woman who looks like this!*

Jessica broke the silence. "It's just like the magazine article said," she murmured. "It's so obvious. That was such a close call back at the airport."

"I can look up those other words in my dictionary," Elizabeth offered halfheartedly.

"Why bother?" Jessica shrugged. "We don't need every word to know exactly what that says."

I know you're right, Elizabeth thought miserably as the twins walked away from the newsstand. *But I sure wish you weren't!*

"It's starting to get dark." Jessica suppressed a shudder. They'd been wandering for what seemed like all day, and now the sun was going down. There was a distinct chill in the air. She thought about pulling a sweatshirt out of her backpack.

"I hope Paris isn't as dangerous after dark as American cities are," Elizabeth said nervously, casting a glance back over her shoulder.

"Me too," Jessica said somberly. Her legs ached, and she stopped outside a storefront to rub them. *I thought Paris at night would be really romantic*, she said to herself. *I thought I'd be zipping around the streets in Alain Monteclaire's car, smelling flowers in the air and hearing music from a hundred different bands.*

And here I am, with a sore leg, running off I-don't-even-know-where, with no place to spend the night, being chased by a cannibal child murderer!

"So much for April in Paris," Jessica said to herself as the shadow of a cloud passed over the sun.

Elizabeth breathed in deeply. "I think we've lucked out in one way."

"What's that?" Jessica asked absentmindedly.

"Smell," Elizabeth commanded. "We're next to a bakery."

Jessica took a cautious sniff, and caught a wonderful sugary aroma. Suddenly she realized she was starving. *What have I eaten since the plane? One stupid croissant.* "Come on," she said to Elizabeth, striding through the door. "What are we waiting for? Let's go have a bite to eat."

"You can't get us on a flight to Paris until next week?" Mrs. Wakefield asked incredulously.

At the airport, a ticket agent clicked away at a keyboard and stared at a computer terminal in front of him. "I'm sorry, ma'am," he said regretfully. "Everything's booked solid. Unless—" He tapped a few more keys. "I could get you there by routing you through, let me see, Sydney and Seoul."

Sydney and Soul!? Steven's ears perked up. Sounds like a new rap group, he thought.

Mr. Wakefield scratched his chin impatiently. "You mean we can only get to Paris if we fly halfway across the world in the wrong direction?"

"More than halfway, actually," the ticket agent told him. "Sydney's in Australia, and Seoul is in Korea." He shrugged. "*It is a little out of your way, but I'm afraid it's all we have.*"

"Australia? Korea?" Mrs. Wakefield bit her lip. "That would take us a couple of days, wouldn't it?"

The agent studied the display on the terminal. "Four days, actually, ma'am," he said at last. "There would be a long layover in Sydney and—" Catching sight of the look on Mrs. Wakefield's face, he stopped. "Or you might like to try another airline."

"I think we'd better." Mr. Wakefield frowned. "Come on, Steven," he said, picking up his carry-on bag. "Let's go."

Steven hefted his backpack. It was stuffed to the seams with T-shirts bearing the names of American colleges. In fact, Steven reminded himself as he fell in line behind his father, his backpack contained half his collection of eighty-six shirts. Too bad he hadn't been able to fit all eighty-six inside. He remembered reading somewhere that American college T-shirts were incredibly hot stuff in Europe.

I'm going to make a killing, he promised himself, his eyes dancing.

"Bonsoir, bonsoir!" Elizabeth called out as they entered the bakery, using the French expression for "good evening."

Somewhere in the back of the store, a man yelled something in French, speaking far too fast for Elizabeth to understand. At the same moment, a cloud of flour billowed toward them from a doorway to a back room. The far wall was full of the dusty white particles. Elizabeth coughed.

"Pardon?" she tried again.

This time a woman shouted something. Another puff of flour wafted through the air.

"What's she saying?" Jessica whispered.

"I don't know," Elizabeth answered. "But she sure sounds mad!"

A tall thin man dressed in white came out of a back room and staggered toward the girls. Elizabeth took a step back. She had never seen anyone so pale.

The man didn't seem to notice them. Instead, he whirled and shouted something into the room behind him. He was still in the middle of a sentence when a third puff of flour hit him directly in the face.

"That's why he's so pale," Elizabeth muttered, seizing Jessica's hand. Together they backed up until they were against the wall. "He's covered with flour!"

The tall man groped inside a pastry case beside him. He pulled out two large jelly doughnuts. Winding his arm back, he threw them into the back room.

"Aaaaah!" a woman screamed.

Elizabeth could tell the doughnuts had found their target.

A young woman stormed into view, purple jelly streaming down her face. She untied an apron from around her waist and threw it at the tall man as she ran past him. Pausing at the front door, she yelled some more words that Elizabeth couldn't catch. Then she darted onto the sidewalk, slamming the door so hard that Elizabeth could feel the floor shake.

"Let's get out of here," Jessica muttered, edging closer to the door herself.

The tall man seemed to notice them for the first time. He grinned widely. "Ah, bonsoir, bonsoir!"

"Uh, bonsoir," Elizabeth said hesitantly, trying to keep herself from laughing. Flour covered the whole upper half of his body, and she thought she could see a bit of egg yolk trickling down from near his ear. He bowed and spoke again.

"What did he say?" Jessica whispered in Elizabeth's ear.

"He asked if he could help us," Elizabeth hissed back.

The baker got a crafty look in his eye. "Ah, you speak English!" he said with a heavy accent. "I knows very good the English, yes?" He smiled broadly, and the egg yolk dripped onto his collar. He gestured toward two floury chairs. "Take please seats," he said, disappearing behind the counter. "Many sorries about what you see. But I make OK. I feed you great samples of my work, yes?"

"Yes!" Jessica exclaimed.

Elizabeth didn't even mind the flour. She dropped her backpack and sank wearily into the nearest chair. "Yes!" she echoed happily.

Great. Just great, Steven thought with exasperation. They'd finally gotten a direct flight to France, but it wouldn't be ready to board for another half hour. The airport chairs were hard, and there really wasn't enough room to stretch out.

He was having a hard time waiting. Visions of the money he'd make from his T-shirts danced in his head. *What could I get?* he wondered. *Say twenty-five bucks for each one—twenty-five bucks for forty-three shirts—three times five was fifteen, carry the one—*Steven wrinkled his forehead and concentrated hard.

Well, a ton of cash, anyway.

Steven opened the battered old copy of *Speak French Just as a Native Might Do. If I'm going to sell my shirts, I'll need some useful phrases,* he thought. He could picture himself haggling with French kids about prices. "Five francs?" he practiced saying aloud. "For *this*? Are you out of your *mind*?" Yeah, it *would* be just like some snotty kid to offer just five francs for my *Southeastern Massachusetts Tech* shirt that's only got *three holes!*

Steven flipped through the book. "Nothing!" he grumbled at last. "Totally *useless!*" He glanced up at his mother. "Hey, Mom, can you believe it? This stupid book doesn't even tell you how to say 'Only worn twice—what a deal, huh?'"

"That's nice, dear," Mrs. Wakefield mumbled, looking distractedly at the list of departing flights a few feet in front of her.

Steven frowned. *Oh, well.* He plunked the book down and headed for the gift shop to buy a pencil and a pad of paper.

Yup, Jessica had the right idea putting together her own phrase book!

"Ze woman zat ran out of ze store was my help-air," the baker sighed. He was sitting at the table with the twins now. "She is quit. Done, gone, fin-ish! It is ze ninth time she has left me—Monsieur Courbet—ze greatest baker in France."

Jessica bit into a chocolate and strawberry pastry and felt the scrumptious mixture slide down her throat. "Ze ninth time?"

Monsieur Courbet nodded. "She quit once, twice each month. But zis one—ah, zis one will ruin me." He reached for a jelly doughnut, his third. Jessica wondered how he managed to stay so thin.

"Why is that?" Elizabeth asked, frowning.

"Ah." Monsieur Courbet gestured wildly with

the jelly doughnut. "We must bake, bake, bake all day long for a wedding. Today we bake, tomorrow we bake. We bake and bake and bake and bake and finally we are done. But I cannot finish ze baking alone," he said mournfully, reaching for another doughnut with his free hand. "And zen I am ruined, ruined, ruined!"

A glimmer of an idea was beginning to come to Jessica. *He needs some help, and we need a place to hide out.* She leaned forward. "You know, I'm an incredibly awesome baker," she said slowly.

Monsieur Courbet looked blank. "'Incredibly awesome,'" he repeated. "Sorry. I do not understand. 'Incredible' means 'cannot be believed,' and 'awesome'—" His face fell into a puzzled frown.

Jessica sighed. In her mind she added "incredibly awesome" to her list of expressions she'd translate for her phrase book. "I mean I'm very good."

"Ah." Monsieur Courbet gave her a wide smile. He took one bite from the doughnut in his left hand, and followed it immediately with a bite from the doughnut in his right hand. "You bake, pair-haps, cookies from a cookie mix in your kitchen, yes?"

"No way!" Jessica shook her head violently. "I mean, no. I baked on national television once."

Monsieur Courbet snickered.

"And I don't just make boring old sugar cookies, either," Jessica continued proudly, trying hard to impress Monsieur Courbet. "I make cookies à la sugar."

"Cookies à la sugar," Monsieur Courbet repeated slowly. "Pray tell, what are—"

Jessica snapped her fingers quickly. "You know," she said, putting on her best smile and resting her arms on the table, "the person we were supposed to stay with got held up out of town for a day or two. Maybe if—"

"Ah!" Monsieur Courbet interrupted, dropping both doughnuts onto the table and jumping to his feet. "I am get great idea! You stay ze night in ze back of ze shop, and in ze morning you help me with—"

"It's a deal!" Jessica broke in, her face lighting up.

"But, Jess—" Elizabeth began, her eyes pleading with her twin's.

Jessica hated to do it, but she saw no way out. Aiming carefully, she kicked her sister squarely in the shin. Hard.

"Ouch!" Elizabeth winced. As she leaned down to rub her leg, Jessica smiled once more at Monsieur Courbet.

"As I was saying, it's a wonderful idea!" she said, pretending to be surprised. "I think that would work just fine!"

"I will go turn ze oven back on!" Monsieur Courbet said, clasping his hands together with excitement. He darted back behind the counter, knocking his chair over in the process.

As soon as the baker was out of earshot, Elizabeth turned to her sister, arms folded. "As I was going to say before you decided to kick me in the shin— Are you totally nuts? You're not that good a cook."

"I baked on national television, remember?" Jessica demanded.

"Well, yes," Elizabeth admitted slowly. "But you're still not exactly an expert or anything." She bit her lip. "What's he going to do when he finds out?"

Jessica snorted. "We'll figure that out when we get there," she said grandly. "And anyway, the point is, now we won't have to sleep in the park." Jessica leaned closer. "Or be stuffed and put under glass."

Elizabeth shuddered involuntarily. She was starting to see Jessica's point.

Seven

"Hey, Dad?" Steven poked his father in the side with the copy of *International Traveler* he was holding. They'd finally boarded their plane and had been up in the air for about half an hour. "Hey, Dad, listen to this!"

Mr. Wakefield turned away from the airplane window. Steven thought his face looked a little pale. "What is it, son?" he asked wearily.

"This is completely unbelievable," Steven said. He opened the magazine and tapped his finger on one of the pages. "According to this article, Johnny Buck's lead drummer only started playing drums when he was *sixteen!*

"Is that right?" Mr. Wakefield swiveled back to the window.

"But, Dad—" Steven stopped in mid-sentence. It was obvious his father wasn't interested. He tried his mother instead. "Hey, Mom," he began, "how about buying me a drum set when we get back home?"

Mrs. Wakefield continued to drum her fingers on the tray in front of her.

Steven sighed. Parents could be such a pain sometimes. "Earth to Mom!" He leaned over and waved his hand in front of her face.

"What is it, Steven?" Mrs. Wakefield turned toward her son, looking startled.

"Johnny Buck's lead drummer didn't start drumming till he was sixteen," Steven repeated. "If I start now, I know I can be better than him. How about it, huh, Mom?"

Mrs. Wakefield blinked. "We'll talk about it when we get home." She looked away and started drumming her fingers again.

Rats. Steven looked from one parent to the other. Then he looked down at the picture of the lead drummer once more. "I *know* I have more talent than that clown," he said to no one in particular. "Besides being better looking."

Steven flipped a few more pages. Perfume ads . . . hotel ads . . . jewelry ads. Suddenly a familiar face caught his eye. *One of the twins!* he thought with surprise. "What's Jessica or Elizabeth doing in this magazine?"

"What's that?" Mrs. Wakefield looked up suddenly.

Steven peered more closely at the picture. No, it definitely wasn't one of his sisters, after all. He realized that, weirdly enough, his heart had been hammering away for a moment there. "I thought I saw the twins in this magazine," Steven explained. "One of them, anyway. But it's somebody else." He showed his mother a photo of a girl standing in front of the Eiffel Tower.

"You're right," Mrs. Wakefield said after a moment. She sounded disappointed. "It's somebody else. They do look alike, though."

"Only this one isn't as dorky," Steven muttered. "And she looks a little less—well, juvenile."

"Steven." Mr. Wakefield raised his eyebrows.

"Sor-ry," Steven muttered, sliding lower into his seat. He scowled. *Whatever happened to free speech?* Anyway, the girl did look more grown-up than his loser little sisters.

Mrs. Wakefield looked over Steven's shoulder at the picture caption. "Ned, listen to this!" she gasped. Grabbing the magazine from Steven's hands, she read aloud. "This American tourist was visiting France last Christmas, when she disappeared near the Bastille.'" She bit her lip and read on. "It says several other American girls have disappeared during the last year. Oh, Ned!"

"You think they've been kidnapped?" Mr. Wakefield frowned and rubbed his forehead. Then he shook his head. "No. Remember, Madame du Noir said they ran away. And they'd better have a darn good excuse," he added under his breath.

"Maybe you're right," Mrs. Wakefield let out her breath.

Steven leaned forward. *Kidnapped, huh?* he thought. The idea sounded kind of interesting. How would the twins act if they were kidnapped?

Steven winced, remembering some of the arguments he'd had with the twins over the years. *Good luck to the kidnapper,* he thought. *If I know my sisters, he's going to need it!*

"Rise and shine!" Monsieur Courbet came scurrying into the little back room, where Elizabeth and Jessica had slept on cots.

Elizabeth sat up, rubbing the sleep from her eyes. To her surprise, Monsieur Courbet's white uniform already seemed to be covered with flour. He turned on the lights and tripped over Jessica's cot. "Time to do ze baking!" he said as he fell heavily against an enormous stove.

"Baking?" Jessica rolled over and groaned. "Who said anything about baking?"

Elizabeth bit her lip as she saw a disbelieving look cover Monsieur Courbet's face. "What a kidder," she broke in quickly, pasting on her biggest and—she hoped—most convincing grin. "Isn't she a riot? Ha ha!"

"A riot?" Monsieur Courbet stared at her in confusion. "A riot are a fight when a great crowd of people shoot one another, no?"

"Umm—no, it's an expression," Elizabeth said quickly. "It just means she's very funny, that's all."

"Ah." Monsieur Courbet pushed himself away from the stove and grinned widely. "A riot. I will remember."

An idea flashed into Elizabeth's mind. *If "riot" is just an American expression, maybe "under glass" means something totally innocent, too.* "She's so silly, sometimes we have to cook her and put her under glass," she told Monsieur Courbet.

"Huh?" Jessica looked wide awake now.

"Excuse me?" Monsieur Courbet said with a frown.

"You know, *under glass*," Elizabeth repeated with emphasis, hoping the words would trigger some association.

Monsieur Courbet's face darkened. "Maybe zat is what you do in America, but here only crazy murder-ers—"

"Just a joke," Elizabeth said quickly, not meeting Jessica's eyes. She'd heard all she wanted to hear.

"Next time we come to Paris," Mr. Wakefield said irritably, "let's try not to use the baggage check—all right, Steven?"

"All right," Steven said, shrugging. They'd arrived at the Paris airport and were waiting for Steven's backpack to emerge from the luggage carousel. Steven had been surprised to find that his parents had only packed carry-on bags themselves.

"But I really wanted to bring along my college T-shirts and—"

"Never mind!" His father scowled. Then he shook his head and managed a grin. "Sorry, Steven. I'm just worried about the girls, that's all."

"No problem," Steven assured him. He wandered to the front of the carousel. *I sure hope the girls show up quickly,* he thought. He hoped to have some time to enjoy Paris—see a soccer game, check out the music, maybe Rollerblade down the Champs

Élysées, which he'd read was the city's main drag.

Thud. Steven bumped into a flight attendant. *Watch where you're going, Wakefield,* he scolded himself. Steven leaned over and picked up the carrying case the woman had dropped. "Pardon, pardon," he said in his best French, handing it back to her.

She smiled as he straightened up. "You have a nice French accent," she said pleasantly in perfect English, taking the case.

Steven squared his shoulders a little more. "Umm, thank you," he said shyly. She was kind of cute, he thought, tall and blond with a nice smile. A little old for him, though—around twenty-five, he guessed. "How'd you know I was an American?"

"By your shirt." The flight attendant pointed to the blue and gold West Central New Mexico Poly shirt that Steven was wearing.

"But I thought college shirts were real popular in Europe," Steven said. "I heard that all the kids here were wearing them."

"That was a few years ago," the flight attendant told him. "Not anymore."

Steven's jaw dropped. "You're kidding me!" *Forty-three T-shirts, lugged all this way—for nothing?*

"I'm Katharine, by the way." The flight attendant's voice broke into his thoughts.

Steven stared at the hand she held out for him. *Shake hands with the lady, Wakefield!* he commanded. They shook hands, and he introduced himself. He felt his face grow warm. *She's really pretty, he thought. And friendly, too.*

"Have you been studying French for long?" Katharine asked brightly.

Steven realized he'd forgotten to let go of her hand. He dropped it quickly and considered the question. *Would it be more impressive to say I started learning it when I was four months old, he wondered. Or that I just started a little while ago? He decided to keep it vague.* "Umm, not very—" He cleared his throat, wishing his voice didn't sound so high-pitched. "Not very long."

"Well, good for you." Katharine smiled. "I bet you'll love Paris. Will you be staying for a while?"

"I hope so," Steven said in his best bass voice. *There, that was better.*

"Awesome!" Katharine nodded vigorously.

Awesome. Katharine's word made him think about his phrase book. "Hey, are you bilingual?" he demanded.

"*Oui, oui, monsieur!*" Katharine dropped a curtsy.

"Oh, good," Steven said. Reaching into his pocket, he pulled out his pad of paper. "How do you say 'These guys won the NCAA Division Three—'" Suddenly he blushed. "I mean," he began again with what he hoped was a little more dignity, "would it be possible for you to help me with a project I'm working on?"

"What kind of project?" Katharine asked, checking her watch.

"Oh, nothing." Steven felt embarrassed. *This was a really stupid idea,* he told himself. "I was just kind of hoping to get some phrases that would be, like, really helpful in France. You know. Make my own phrase book or something." Wrinkling his nose, he studied the ground in front of him. *She'll probably tell me that's a dippy idea,* he thought gloomily. *I should never have mentioned it.*

"That's strange." Katharine spoke as if to herself.

"What?" Steven looked at her curiously.

"There was a girl doing that same project on my flight yesterday morning," Katharine said slowly. She stared hard at Steven.

Steven's mouth felt dry. "That would have been my sister, Jessica," he managed to get out. "Umm, did she look, you know, kind of dorky?"

"Dorky?" Katharine frowned.

Steven cleared his throat and tried to figure out another way to describe his sister. It was strange how other people didn't automatically recognize Jessica's true dorkiness. "Umm, well, was she with a girl who looked exactly like her?"

"Totally identical," Katharine said promptly. "They were your sisters? But you were flying on a different plane. They didn't say you were coming to join them."

"Well, I wasn't really supposed to," Steven began. "Hey—uh, Katharine—" It felt awkward to call an adult by her first name. "Did Jessica seem, you know, nervous or anything when you talked to her?"

"You could say that," Katharine agreed. "She was worried about the woman they were going to be staying with—Madame du . . ." She frowned.

"Du Noir," Steven supplied, his pulse quicken-

ing. Maybe that's why they ran away! he thought. What idiots. A stupid letter says she's a fiend instead of a friend, and she doesn't have a really cute older brother, so they head for the hills. Typical girls. Afraid of a little old—

"Of course, I'd be shocked if it was the same woman," Katharine said, looking worriedly into the distance.

Steven studied Katharine's face. What was she talking about? "What woman?"

"The old woman in Paris who's been kidnapping young girls," Katharine said with a frown. "I'm sure it's not this Madame du Noir, but your sisters might've jumped to that conclusion."

"Oh," Steven said, feeling a little nervous.

"It would probably send Jessica over the edge altogether," Katharine sighed. "A great kid, but, well, a little young. You seem a little more—you know, mature."

"Yeah, well," Steven said modestly. His anxiety was quickly dissolving, and his heart was thumping with delight. *Check it out!* he told himself. *Wakefield, the man!*

Katharine checked her watch once more. "Oops, it's almost time for my flight back to L.A. Nice to meet you, Steven." She offered her hand once more. "Will you be seeing your sisters in Paris?"

"Umm, I hope so," Steven said.

"Well, tell them I said hello and not to worry, OK?" Katharine waved and disappeared into the crowd.

Whoa, baby! Steven drew a long, shuddering breath. "You seem a little more mature," he quoted.

His gaze followed Katharine until she disappeared from view.

Oo la la! he thought, a goofy grin spreading across his face.

I think I'm in love!

Eight

"Zhessica!" Monsieur Courbet sounded exasperated.

"Yes, sir." Humbly Jessica held out the mixing bowl. "But I don't understand. I put ten cups of flour in with the eggs, like you said—"

"Not wiss ze eggs!" Monsieur Courbet gritted his teeth and made a gesture toward the ceiling. "You have ruined it. Ze flour must not get wet until it is time, do you not see?"

Jessica looked at the soggy mixture at the bottom of the bowl. It did look pretty unappetizing, she had to admit. She swirled the bowl to mix the ingredients a little better. But it didn't seem to improve things much.

"First ze baking powder must be added," Monsieur Courbet said, gesturing to the stove. "Zen ze sugar, what your sister are so carefully mixing over zere. Zen and only zen comes ze eggs!" He took a deep breath. "And you say you have baked on television. What was ze show—*Stupid Teenager Tricks?*"

"Umm, I'm really sorry, Monsieur Courbet," Jessica said gloomily. "Still—" She knew she should just shut up, but she tried one last time to defend herself. "I really thought you told me to pour the flour in the bowl with the eggs."

"Not ze bowl with ze eggs!" Monsieur Courbet roared, hopping up and down and nearly splitting his head on a low beam in the ceiling. "Ze bowl with ze *ecks!*"

With the ecks? Jessica repeated to herself, wondering frantically what in the world an eck was. She cast an anxious glance over to Elizabeth, who stood in the corner measuring sugar. Elizabeth shrugged, a bleak expression on her face. "I'm sorry, Monsieur Courbet," Jessica tried again. "But what are ecks?"

"Ecks! Ecks! Ecks!" He snorted, hitting his fist into his palm. "You know—ze letter zat come after double-you and before why!"

"'X,'" Jessica groaned as she realized what Monsieur Courbet meant. "The bowl with the 'x' on it." She put her hand to her mouth. On the counter she could plainly see a large yellow mixing bowl with a big 'x' carved into the side. "Oh, Monsieur Courbet, I'm so sorry. . . ."

"Never mind," he told her, covering his head with his hands. "I do it myself. But I give one chance more. Put zis in ze oven. Burn it!" He handed her a baking pan with a few small loaves inside.

Burn it? "Umm . . . Monsieur Courbet?" Jessica hesitated. "You don't really want me to burn it, do you?"

"Yes, I want you to burn it!" Monsieur Courbet shouted, his eyes glittering. "For loud crying, do you not speak ze English so good or somezing? Put it in ze oven, turn ze oven up high, and burn it!"

Jessica gulped. *He must mean "make it very hot" or something,* she thought. "Umm, how hot, Monsieur Courbet?"

The baker sank down into a chair. Unfortunately it was covered with a pan of rolls he had just pulled from the oven. "Ouch!" he cried, springing up suddenly. "Put it on, let me see, two hundred for temperature will be a success." He turned his back to Jessica and strode out of the room.

Two hundred degrees? Jessica bit her lip. Two hundred degrees wasn't nearly enough to bake anything, even she knew that. *You bake chocolate chip cookies at almost twice that.* Sighing, she placed the pans in the oven and turned the heat up to the highest marking she could find. "Four hundred and fifty degrees ought to do it," she murmured, shaking her head.

"This isn't going to work," Elizabeth hissed. Jessica turned. Her sister's eyes looked as though they were trying to hold back tears. Elizabeth set her measuring cup down and tried to smile. "I'm trying, Jessica, really I am, but I can't do this!"

"Of course you can," Jessica said a little unsteadily. "It's simple. You just dip in the cup and—"

"But what happens if I forget how many times?"

Elizabeth asked. She pointed to the sugar lying in the bowl beside her. "And he didn't tell me if I was supposed to measure the cupfuls level, or if I was supposed to make them heaping, or what."

Jessica patted her twin's back. "Just do the best you can."

"And then he said something about using the black sugar, and I don't know what he means!" Elizabeth went on desperately. "I thought maybe he was talking about brown sugar, but he definitely said black. What should I do?"

Black sugar? Jessica wrinkled her nose and tried to think.

"Six cakes are too many to bake at one time, anyway," Elizabeth continued. "I mean, let's face it, Jess, even one cake is too many for us."

"It's not that bad," Jessica said, hoping that it really wasn't. "Here. Why don't I help you?" She reached for the measuring cup. "How many cupfuls were there supposed to be, anyway?"

"He said eighty." Elizabeth twisted her shirt in her hands.

"Eighty?" Jessica licked her lips and looked down at the humongous mound of sugar in front of her. "That sounds like a lot. Doesn't it sound like a lot to you?"

"I thought so." Elizabeth brushed a small cloud of flour away from her eyes. "But then I thought maybe it was a really enormous cake."

Jessica examined the pile of sugar critically. "I think you could feed all of Paris with what you've got already. Listen, Lizzie!" An idea had just struck her. "Do you think he maybe said eighteen instead of eighty?"

"I don't know." Behind a layer of flour, Elizabeth's face looked thin and pinched. "I thought he said eighty."

"Well, we'll ask him when he comes back," Jessica decided. "His English isn't as good as he thinks it is, you know."

"Yeah, but my French isn't as good as I thought it was, either," Elizabeth said unhappily. She sniffed the air. "What's that awful smell?"

Jessica held up her nose and took a deep breath. "Something does smell pretty bad," she said after a pause. She sniffed again, a little more delicately this time. "I think it's coming from that oven." Her heart sank. *The oven where I just put those loaves a few minutes ago!*

"You'd better check it," Elizabeth said with a worried expression on her face. But before Jessica could move, Monsieur Courbet dashed back into the kitchen.

"What is *now* ze problem?" he gasped, flinging open the oven door. Thick black smoke poured out.

"Yuk!" Jessica said, blinking to avoid the acrid fumes.

"My bread!" Monsieur Courbet wailed, pulling out the baking pan and thrusting it quickly into the sink. "What has happened?" He peered at the temperature dial. "Four hundred and fifty degrees!" he shouted, clutching his chest.

"I thought you wanted them burned," Jessica said meekly. "And besides, you can't bake anything at two hundred degrees. I mean—"

"Um, Jess?" Elizabeth interrupted in a strangled voice. "I think he meant Celsius. We measure temperature in degrees Fahrenheit, but in France they use a different system. Two hundred degrees here would be, like, four hundred back home."

"Oh, man." Jessica's heart wasn't just sinking any more. By now it was in free fall. Without a parachute. "So when I set it at four-fifty—"

"Maybe eight hundred degrees." Elizabeth bit her lip.

"Oh, man," Jessica said again. She sniffed the air and gagged. *No wonder.*

Monsieur Courbet motioned to Elizabeth. "You!" he barked. "Come fill zis bag wiss frosting! And you!" he called to Jessica. "In ze office are more flour. Fetch!"

Jessica ran to the office. *This isn't going to work,* she thought miserably. There were too many problems. Starting with the fact that she'd forgotten how it had taken at least a gazillion tries before she'd gotten the sugar cookies right for the TV show.

She pulled herself up short. There on the desk in front of her was a phone.

A phone! *I can call the U.S. and let Mom and Dad know what's going on!* Jessica kicked herself. Why hadn't she thought of that before? For the first time all day, Jessica smiled. Lifting the receiver, she punched buttons furiously. "Monsieur Courbet won't like it," she mumbled guiltily. "But, hey. This is a matter of life and death." *And if it isn't now, it will be once he gets his phone bill.*

After what seemed like eternity, the phone began to ring. *Twice . . . three times . . . four.* There was a metallic click. Jessica groaned. "Great," she muttered. "I've gotten the machine."

Steven's voice blasted her eardrums. "Hello!" he said brightly. "My dippy sisters are in France and—"

Well, so much for that idea. Jessica sighed and hung up.

"And when I turn to look, Monsieur Oo-ake-feel, zey were vanish!" Madame du Noir motioned excitedly across the breakfast table at Mr. and Mrs. Wakefield. "I am try to follow in taxi, but in Centre Pompidou, I am lose zem again." She twisted her napkin and reached for her coffee cup.

Steven studied her critically. They'd been with Madame du Noir at the restaurant in their hotel for the last fifteen minutes. *She's kind of old,* Steven thought, *but she sure doesn't seem like anyone to be frightened of!*

Sure, Madame du Noir was dressed mostly in black. And she hadn't smiled an awful lot. Steven tried to think of a word that would describe her. There was some word they used in books a lot to describe old-maid teachers who were kind of strict.

"So I am call police," Madame du Noir went on, "but zey are saying we must wait two-and-seventy hours before zey put out alarm—"

Severe, that was it. Steven stretched. *Madame du Noir looked pretty severe. Not a whole lot of fun. But not someone to run away from, either!* He sighed and wondered if he could order another chocolate éclair. Maybe two.

"I also am putting airplanes around ze city," Madame du Noir said.

Steven stiffened. "Airplanes?" he asked.

Madame du Noir waved her hand in the air. "Airplanes," she repeated. "You are surely knowing. But pair-haps I have wrong word, yes? Zey are pay-pairs with your sis-tairs' names——"

Airplanes. Steven grinned. "You mean flyers."

"Yes, of course, flyers," Madame du Noir agreed. "Zey will hang on every street corner in Paris. We will find zose daugh-tairs of yours, Madame Oo-ake-feel. I am promise!" She looked earnestly at them.

"Well, what are we waiting for?" Mr. Wakefield stood up briskly. "Madame du Noir, I can't thank you enough for your help. We'd better start posting those flyers. Come on, Steven."

Steven scowled. *But what about my plans for the day?* he thought, fingering the bulging backpack at his feet. Reluctantly he dragged himself upright.

"Tie-aired?" Madame du Noir asked him, a grin on her lips.

Tie-aired? Steven thought blankly. *Tie*——"Oh!" he said, suddenly understanding. "Yeah. I guess I am a little tired. It was kind of a long flight." He hoisted up his backpack.

"Ze one cure for being tie-aired," Madame du Noir told him, wiggling her finger in front of his face, "zat is exercise. Exercise! Hanging up zese airplanes, zat will be ze goodest exercise for you, yes?" She handed him a stack of blue papers. The words "Jesica" and "Elizabet" jumped out at him.

"Umm . . ." he began bleakly. *Hanging up flyers all day long is not exactly what I had in mind,* he wanted to say.

"Good for you!" Madame du Noir said happily, clapping Steven on the back.

Steven sighed loudly as they walked out to the street. *Well, if I can't have a real vacation here in Paris till we find them,* he thought, *I guess I'll just have to find them myself, that's all.* The idea of being a hero made him grin all over. He nodded to himself, imagining his parents' reaction as he kind of casually brought his sisters back to the hotel. "Oh, by the way, here they are, Dad," he'd say, leading them into the room. "Oh, my gosh!" his father would say, springing up from his seat. "How on earth did you do it?" He'd shake Steven's hand and offer him the keys to the family van. And his mother would say something like, "It sure is nice to have one kid who's old enough to take care of himself!"

And then maybe I could have a couple of days to hang out—Rollerblade and all that.

Yup. Steven nodded again. Finding the girls himself, that was the ticket.

And if I know my sisters, he thought, a grin playing at the corners of his mouth, *there are a few obvious places to look!*

"Is this how it works?" Elizabeth pulled doubtfully at one end of a cloth bag.

"Just like," Monsieur Courbet assured her, scowling. "Ze frosting goes in *here*"—he motioned to one end of the bag with a finger—"and you squeeze *here*, and write on ze cake. Can you do it?"

Elizabeth stared up at the tall, thin baker in front of her. He was covered with all sorts of stains from baking six wedding cakes. *Chocolate above his right ear*, she thought, *and lemon all over his left knee—and flour, flour everywhere.*

Under any other circumstances, Elizabeth would have laughed. But not today. "I—I think so," she stammered. She was beginning to understand why Monsieur Courbet's assistant had quit nine times already. Grabbing one end of the frosting bag, she squeezed hard.

"Not like zat!" Monsieur Courbet screeched.

A stream of pale blue frosting squirted out of the nozzle and cascaded down Monsieur Courbet's right leg. Backing up quickly, the baker bumped into the counter, knocking three cake layers onto the floor. Elizabeth tried to stop herself, but she couldn't seem to send the right message to her hands. The blue icing kept pouring out—onto the floor, onto the cake, and all over Monsieur Courbet, who by now was bouncing around the kitchen screaming at the top of his lungs.

Jessica came running back into the room. "Sheesh!" she said to Elizabeth, rolling her eyes and snatching the frosting bag away. "What do you think you're doing, huh?"

"I tried to stop it," Elizabeth said, tears welling in her eyes, "but I couldn't. Honestly, Jess, it's not my fault! I've never used one of these things before!"

"But you have baked cookies à la sugar!" Monsieur Courbet looked even more ridiculous than before, his pants covered with pale blue frosting.

"How you make zis silly mistake?" he thundered.

Jessica stepped in front of Elizabeth protectively. "Don't yell at my sister like that, please," she said fiercely. "And for your information, you don't use frosting when you make cookies."

Monsieur Courbet looked as if he might have more to say, but instead he bit his lip. "Very well." He sighed heavily. "Here is sponge. Please mop ze floor. I cannot have blue icing all over my floor."

"I'm really sorry," Elizabeth said, accepting the sponge. "I—I just didn't know—I mean—" She gulped. "Do you want me to wash your uniform, too?"

"My uniform?" Monsieur Courbet drew himself up to his full height and stared down at Elizabeth haughtily. "And what, pray tell, is ze matter wiss my uniform?"

Elizabeth took a deep breath. "Well—" she began. But Monsieur Courbet had disappeared into the main room of the bakery.

"I tried calling home," Jessica said softly, bending toward her sister as Elizabeth slowly filled the sponge with water.

Elizabeth's heart leaped. *What a great idea!* "And?" she asked, trying to keep her voice steady.

"And nothing." Jessica shrugged sadly. "All I got was the machine."

Elizabeth soaped up one corner of the floor. Luckily the icing seemed to come up pretty easily.

Unfortunately there was kind of a lot of it. "So you left a message?"

"No." Jessica shook her head. "What would we say?"

"Hmm." Elizabeth considered. "How about something like 'Mom, Dad, help! Madame du Noir is a kidnapper and a murderer, and you can reach us at—'" She sighed. "I guess you're right. They'd probably think it was a joke or something."

"If our darling brother didn't erase the message by accident," Jessica put in. "We'll just have to try again later." She grabbed a sponge and knelt by Elizabeth.

For a few minutes they cleaned in silence. "I wonder if we shouldn't just turn ourselves in," Elizabeth said at last.

"Turn ourselves in?" Jessica stared at her, her mouth open. "Why in the world would we want to do a crazy thing like that?"

"Well, we can't stay here!" Elizabeth argued. "Monsieur Courbet's got us figured out by now, and it isn't fair for us to ruin the wedding by baking inedible cakes." She put her sponge to one side and stared morosely at the layer cake on the floor. "I wonder if Madame du Noir really did say that 'under glass' stuff. I wonder if I just didn't hear it right. Like when the guy said 'croissant' and I thought he was saying 'fish.'"

Jessica rolled her eyes. "Like, what do you think you might have heard?"

"Well," Elizabeth began. She racked her brain, trying to think of something that sounded a little like the French word for 'glass.'" "Like . . ." She hesitated. "Umm, maybe—I mean—"

"Bonjour, bonjour!" Monsieur Courbet's voice boomed from the main room in the bakery. Elizabeth looked questioningly at her sister.

"He's got a customer, that's all," Jessica told her impatiently. "Go on."

"Bonjour!" a woman replied from the next room, and then launched into a flurry of French.

Elizabeth stared at her sister, every muscle in her body tensing up. "I know that voice!" she hissed, and by the look on her sister's face she could tell that Jessica did, too.

Madame du Noir!

Nine

◇

Six more flyers to go. Steven wiped his sweaty forehead and tacked another one in place on the telephone pole in front of him. "Where's Madame du Noir?" he asked, stepping back to see if the flyer was straight.

"She went into that bakery across the street," Mrs. Wakefield answered. "Move it a little to the left, Steven."

Steven did as he was told. "Is she going to get pastries for me?"

"For all of us, Steven," Mr. Wakefield said. "Tell you what. You hang up these last ones, and we'll bring some food out to you."

"All right." Steven squinted up at the hot sun. He wished he'd brought along his shades. "Make mine an éclair. Actually, two éclairs. Definitely one of the chocolate and raspberry ones, OK?"

There was no answer. His father had already hurried away.

"Well, thank you for your input, Steven," Steven muttered to no one in particular. He moved to the other side of the telephone pole. Every muscle in his body ached.

That Madame du Noir is something else, he thought admiringly, remembering the way she'd led his family across Paris. *Who'd have thought the old girl had so much life in her? You'd think she was way too old for this stuff.* He wrinkled his nose and stretched to hang another flyer. *How old is she, I wonder? Past fifty, anyway.*

"What is going on?"

Steven looked down. A boy about his own age stood staring at the flyer. "Are they your friends?" he asked, with only a trace of a French accent.

"Sisters," Steven explained. "They just plain took off when they got here yesterday. You seen them or something?"

"I? No," the boy replied. "Sorry."

Steven looked at the boy carefully. "So how'd you know I spoke English?"

The boy grinned. "Your shirt," he said. "Only American kids would wear something like that these days."

Steven had a sinking feeling in his stomach. It was terrible being a few years behind the times. "Really?" he asked sheepishly. "Someone told me that, but—"

"You've heard it right. They're not cool here anymore." The boy glanced at the pack on Steven's back. "What is in there?" he asked curiously.

"Oh—umm—nothing much," Steven said,

embarrassed. He decided to change the subject. "Hey, have you ever heard the expression 'way cool' before?"

"Sure." The boy nodded. "It's the title of one of Johnny Buck's songs."

Steven started. *How come Johnny Buck songs make it over here—but not college T-shirts?* He sighed over the unfairness of it all. "You listen to Johnny Buck a lot?"

The boy shrugged. "When it is possible. His recordings are hard to find here in Europe."

Well, how do you like that! Steven scowled down at the ground. *Obviously I should have packed all my Buckster tapes instead!*

"Way cool," the boy repeated. "That one, I have my own copy. The song where the lead drummer really cuts loose. Did you never hear it?"

"Oh, sure," Steven said importantly. "Way coo-ool!'" he sang, mimicking a guitar with his hands. "'I said, Wa-ay coo-ool!' I don't much like the drums in that one, though."

"Really?" the French boy asked with interest. "I'd say that guy's got real talent."

"You're crazy," Steven said automatically. "Anyway, how would you say 'way cool' in French?" He whipped the notepad out of his pocket and pulled a pencil from behind his ear.

"Oh, that's easy," the boy told him. "*Vrai froide.*"

"*Vrai* what?" Steven asked, frowning.

The boy laughed. "I was teasing you. That means, literally, 'very cold.' If you want to be really slangy you have to say 'formidable.'" He turned to go. "Good luck finding your sisters."

"Thanks!" Steven called after him. As he turned to the next telephone pole, he caught sight of two figures scurrying down the street a block away. Funny, he thought with a start, *they look almost like the twins.* Each figure wore a backpack and carried a flight bag in her hand. Both of them were blond, and—

Well, they do look a little paler than my sisters, he thought. *Actually, really white. Still . . .*

"Steven!" His mother called to him excitedly from the door of the bakery.

Reluctantly, Steven took his eyes off the figures down the street. "Coming!" he called, sprinting across the road.

Couldn't have been the girls, he told himself.
That would be too much of a coincidence.

"What an awful coincidence!" Elizabeth said, her heart pounding. Her backpack flounced as she half walked, half ran down the narrow sidewalk. She knew she must have looked ridiculous, covered head to toe with flour, but she didn't care. "Did you hear what she said?"

"Umm . . ." Jessica began. She shook her head. "I guess I didn't."

Elizabeth turned right at a corner. "She walked into the bakery and said to Monsieur Courbet, 'I am out to get two children.'"

Jessica bit her lip and scampered across the street right at Elizabeth's heels. "She said she was out to get us?"

"Uh-huh." Elizabeth paused. *Turn again, or keep going straight?* She decided it didn't matter—the point was to get away from Monsieur Courbet's shop as fast as possible. "Something like that, anyway."

Jessica gave a low whistle. "That's terrible."

"You said it." Elizabeth caught a quick glimpse of herself in a shop window. *I look pretty awful,* she decided, surveying her messy hair, her slept-in clothes, and the smudges of blue icing that covered her shoes. *But the important thing is, we're away from Madame du Noir again!*

Jessica hurried to catch up. "I don't understand how she knew where we were."

"Who knows?" Elizabeth grabbed her flight bag a little tighter to keep it from banging against her knees.

"Maybe she's psychic," Jessica suggested fearfully. "Then we're in big trouble."

"If she's psychic, then we'd better find a really good hiding place," Elizabeth corrected her. "And keep changing it whenever we need to."

"Easy to say," Jessica muttered.

"Anyway," Elizabeth continued, "then Madame du Noir said, 'I am their mother.' And that's when I poked you and said we'd better get out fast."

"Oh, is that what she said?" Jessica asked. "I thought I heard something about how she wanted to choke us with a pear."

"Choke us with a pear?" Elizabeth repeated in a squeaky voice. She stopped short and studied her sister's face. True, her sister didn't know French very well, but Elizabeth felt a new tingle of fear. First 'put them under glass,' then 'choke them with a pear' . . . What next?

Elizabeth sank onto a bench. "I guess we're far enough away from the bakery by now," she said doubtfully. "I feel a little guilty about abandoning Monsieur Courbet, but I guess we didn't have much of a choice."

"You can say that again," Jessica said emphatically. "I am out to get two children. I am their mother,' she quoted with a shudder. "I am going to choke them with a pear." She shook her head. "Anyway, so what now?"

An idea occurred to Elizabeth. Quickly she rummaged in her backpack. "Ha!" she said as she pulled out a guidebook and a map of Paris. "I know just the place!"

"They're here, Steven! They're here!" Mrs. Wakefield sounded so happy, Steven thought she might cry. She led Steven into the bakery. "Can you believe it?"

"Huh?" Steven frowned.

"Never mind the rest of the flyers," his mother said with a wave of her hand. "Isn't it amazing? Madame du Noir came into the bakery and said—well, let's let her tell it. Madame?"

Madame du Noir was standing against the counter, beaming. Behind her stood one of the strangest-looking men Steven had ever seen in his life. Tall and thin, he looked like he'd been rolling in chocolate, flour, and eggs. There was something on one leg that might once have been a strawberry, and as for the other leg—

Steven shuddered. He'd never seen so much blue frosting in his life.

"Elizabeth and Jessica are *here*?" he asked incredulously, looking around. On second thought, maybe it wasn't such a crazy idea. The bakery reminded him a little bit of Jessica's room.

Madame du Noir nodded proudly. "Yes, yes, ze twins!"

The baker grinned. "Gold hair, blue eyes. Both!"

"I am come into zis shop," Madame du Noir began, "and I say Madame du Noir are here to look for two cheeldren and has zis gentleman seen zem—"

"And zen she says," the baker interrupted, "their mother is here, too—"

"And I tell what zese cheeldren look like—" Madame du Noir interrupted again.

"And I say, yes, yes, zey are here!" the baker announced proudly. "Zey were being my help-airs. Ha ha!" He laughed hollowly. "What a riot."

Steven looked around the place. It did look like someone had been having a riot in the bakery.

"Isn't that wonderful, Steven?" His father grasped his shoulder.

Steven was about to answer when suddenly the front door burst open and a young woman dashed up to the counter. Steven's eyes shifted from the woman to the baker and back as they carried on a long and excited conversation in French.

"Zis woman is his assistant," Madame du Noir

translated as they talked. "She are quit yes-tair-day. He have much to do—now she say she want job back."

The baker raised his head. "Take your daughtairs," he told Mr. and Mrs. Wakefield. "I am no longer needing zem. And if you want my advice—give zem baking lessons!" He rolled his eyes.

Steven stifled a laugh. If the baker's uniform was any indication, *he* was the one who needed the baking lessons.

"Oh, girls!" The baker shouted into the back room of the store. "Your parents is here! You can come out now!"

There was a silence. Steven craned his neck to try to see into the room.

"Of all the amazing coincidences," Mrs. Wakefield said happily.

Coincidence. Steven remembered having used that word not so long ago, when he saw those two pale figures running down the street. "Umm . . . ," he began, a hollow feeling at the pit of his stomach. "Uh, sir?"

"Monsieur Courbet am calling Zhessica and Elizabeth!" the baker hollered. "Are you living?" Mr. and Mrs. Wakefield exchanged worried looks.

Steven nervously shifted his weight from one foot to the other. "Maybe I'll—I'll go . . . umm . . . tell them to get a move-on," he said weakly, then dashed past the counter and into the back room, his parents at his heels.

No one was there. Nor were there any backpacks or flight bags, Steven realized with a sinking heart. But someone had been in the room, he was sure—and not so long ago, either.

Because a single shaky word had been written in blue icing on the wall:

"Merci!"

Ten

"Ever since I was little," Elizabeth said with excitement, "I've been wanting to go see the Louvre."

"You would," Jessica said, poking her sister. "Seriously, Lizzie, I think this was a great idea. Lockers to put our stuff in—"

"Crowds to get lost in," Elizabeth added, her eyes dancing mischievously as they ducked behind a school group.

"And besides," Jessica continued, "anybody would know that an art museum is the least likely place to find us. Me, anyway." She snickered. "If Madame du Noir's expecting to find us in the shopping malls of Paris, she's got another thing coming. Of course, I would *much* rather be in the shopping malls of Paris."

Elizabeth wrinkled her nose and took a left turn at the end of the hall.

"Where are we going?" Jessica asked.

Elizabeth grinned. "To see something amazingly awesome."

"Here?" Jessica asked incredulously. She frowned at the statues and paintings that lined the hallways. "I mean, these are nice and all, I mean, if you like that kind of thing. But amazingly awesome?" She shook her head violently. "Not!"

"Not these." Elizabeth dashed around a corner and into a dimly lit room. A crowd of tourists pressed quietly up toward a single painting that hung on the wall. "This one!"

Jessica blinked. "I've seen this before," she said slowly, trying to figure out exactly where. "On a commercial, I think? Or maybe it was the back of a cereal box—"

Elizabeth laughed and pushed her sister forward through the crowd. "It's the *Mona Lisa!*"

"Oh, wow," Jessica said sarcastically, recognizing the painting at last. "The *Mona Lisa!* Gee, I don't know if my heart can stand the thrill." Even so, she stared up at the dark canvas in front of her.

"Isn't it exciting?" Elizabeth whispered.

Jessica studied the painting critically. It was of an ordinary woman with a little half smile on her face. "Exciting isn't exactly the word I'd use," she said, pretending to yawn.

"But it's the *Mona Lisa,*" Elizabeth insisted, her voice quiet with awe.

"And I'm *Jessica Wakefield,*" Jessica said, imitating Elizabeth's hushed tones. "I mean, she isn't even pretty! What's all the fuss about?"

A man in front of Jessica turned around to glare at her.

"One of the most famous paintings of all time, the *Mona Lisa* was created by Leonardo da Vinci in 1503," Elizabeth read from the guidebook in her hands. "You would be hard-pressed to identify his model at sight; whatever his other talents, it seems that Leonardo was not much good at drawing faces—'"

Jessica suppressed a snort. "That's for sure."

Elizabeth closed the guidebook. "Be serious," she told her sister. "Don't you think it's neat to see such a great painting close up like this?"

Jessica peered once more at the *Mona Lisa*. A *not-very-pretty woman*, she thought, *wearing boring clothes, painted by a guy who couldn't do faces. And Lizzie thinks it's neat?*

"You want an honest answer?" she asked, shaking her head. *That's easy.*

"No way!"

Rollerblades—jet skis—maybe bungee jumping?

Steven loped off down the sidewalk in the direction he'd seen the twins heading. If he knew those girls, he knew where to look. *Yup. They might be scared of harmless old Madame du Noir, but they wouldn't pass up an adventure.*

Steven took a right at the first corner. Too bad he hadn't told his parents where he was going, but there just hadn't been time.

Explaining would have taken too long. Anyway, Madame du Noir would never have been able to keep up.

Let's see—left or right? Try left this time. A horn sounded by Steven's ear. Instinctively he jumped, missing a car by three inches. *Where did that guy come from?* Steven asked himself, checking to make sure he was still in one piece. The drivers here seemed even worse than in L.A.

"Well, Mom and Dad'll just have to deal," Steven told himself. "I'll find them sooner or later." *After I find the twins, of course. Anyway, I can figure out* how *to get around this burg, no problemo!*

The street Steven was on curved around to the left. At the next intersection, he decided to get his bearings from an old man sitting on a bench. "Hey!" Steven greeted him, trying to remember his French. "Umm, have you, umm, regardezed two, I mean, deux, umm"—*darn it, what was French for girl?*—"umm, deux filles running this way?"

The old man looked blank. "Zey're about zis high," Steven added, indicating his chest. "Deux of them." He held up two fingers. "Deux filles. Have you regardezed them?"

The man just stared.

"Never mind!" Steven ran on, wishing he knew the French words for "Where's the best place to go Rollerblading around here?"

Oh well. Add it to the list!

*   *   *

"So what's so great about Venus de Milo, anyway?"

Jessica lounged on a chair in the museum coffee shop. Elizabeth looked across at her and sipped a hot chocolate. "Well, you see, Jess," she began, "the statue of Venus de Milo is one of the greatest pieces of art in the world—"

"Yeah, but why?" Jessica interrupted, gesturing with her own cup. "I mean, the woman doesn't even have any arms!"

"But that's part of the point—" Elizabeth stopped abruptly. *What's the use?* she thought. *I'll teach pigs to fly before I can teach my sister to appreciate great art!* She smiled at Jessica. "Have you seen anything here that you've liked?" she asked.

Jessica scratched her head. "The hot chocolate?" Elizabeth set her cup down onto the table with a giggle. "You're impossible," she teased. "But I'm glad you like the hot chocolate. They cost a lot more than I thought they would."

"Hmm." Jessica drained her last drop. "Whatever they cost, it's worth it. Do you think . . ." She cast a meaningful glance at the counter.

"No, I don't," Elizabeth said firmly. "We're kind of low on money."

"Oh, money," Jessica said airily, waving her cup in the air. "Money isn't everything, you know. Take the Venus de Milo. I bet she had tons of money, and look at her now!"

"What's that supposed to mean?" Elizabeth asked warily.

"Standing in a corner of a dusty old art museum," Jessica continued, "without even any arms!"

Stupid fools, Steven thought, angry at the people who had planned Paris.

After running for what seemed like half an hour, getting farther and farther from the bakery all the time, Steven had suddenly rounded a corner and come face to face with—the bakery again. *Must be all these dumb curving streets or something,* Steven thought, rolling his eyes. *I know it's not my fault, anyway.*

"There you are!" Mrs. Wakefield came out of the bakery and hugged her son. "I thought—well, we thought you'd disappeared, too."

Mr. Wakefield stared disapprovingly at Steven's sweaty forehead. "Did you really think this was a sensible time to go for a jog?" he demanded.

"I wasn't jogging!" Steven protested. "I was just—" But the adults were all beginning to move on, so he didn't bother to finish his sentence. *Stupid fools,* he thought, this time glaring in the direction of his mother and father.

"Where else should we look, then?" Mrs. Wakefield sounded worried. "To be so close, and then to lose them at the last moment . . ."

"I know," Mr. Wakefield comforted her. "I guess we could try the shopping malls, or something."

"A bungee-jumping place," Steven suggested.

"Ah, I have it!" Madame du Noir's eyes glittered in the sunshine. "Vair is ze least likely place for zem to go?"

The least likely place? Steven frowned and exchanged glances with his mother. "Umm, probably an art museum or something," he said at last, remembering the conversation he'd had with the twins the day before they'd left. "That is, if Jessica has anything to say about it."

Madame du Noir spread out her arms as wide as they would go. "Zen zat is vair zey are," she said simply. "Ze least likely place. I am remember from when I am little girl. We must try ze Louvre."

"The Louvre." Mrs. Wakefield turned to her husband. "That makes some sense, doesn't it?"

You bet, Steven thought, sizing Madame du Noir up once more. *Not a bad idea at all!* He nodded slowly and studied her face intently.

Pretty impressive for an old coot.

"If I don't have another pastry this minute," Jessica said with determination, "I will probably die." Elizabeth looked at her sister pleadingly. "We just can't afford another pastry, Jess—don't you understand?"

"A pastry costs less than a funeral," Jessica reminded her twin. "I think I'm wasting away." She squeezed the flesh on her side, remembering some of the paintings of very fat naked ladies they had seen in the museum. "See? I've lost about twenty pounds already."

"Sorry," Elizabeth said more firmly. "I don't care

if you've lost thirty pounds, we are not having another pastry."

"I didn't say *we* were having another pastry," Jessica said quickly. "I said *I* was having another pastry. Can I get you anything while I'm up?" She stood and pushed her chair away from the table.

"Jessica!" Elizabeth frowned and pushed her own chair back even more vigorously.

Jessica slowly sat back down again. "OK, OK," she mumbled. *I wish Mom was here,* she thought sadly. *Mom would know what to do. Mom would probably even let me buy a croissant.* "I wish someone would answer the phone at home," she said aloud. Picking up a few leftover crumbs, she set them carefully onto her tongue. "We've tried, what, twice now since we got here, and we just keep getting the machine."

"Maybe it's time to leave a message," Elizabeth said without much conviction.

"Maybe," Jessica agreed. "Hey! What time is it there, anyway?"

Elizabeth considered. "I'm not really sure," she said. "It's six hours' time difference. Unless it's eight." She drummed her fingers on the table top. "Or nine."

"Say seven hours." Jessica counted on her fingers. "Past eleven o'clock—maybe they're asleep, Lizzie."

"I don't know." Elizabeth frowned. "Do you add hours, or do you subtract them?"

Both girls sighed heavily.

Well, one thing's for sure, Jessica thought as she scanned the crowds of people parading through the museum.

I'm not looking at any more paintings of fat naked ladies!

Eleven

The least likely place. Steven consulted his tourist map of the Louvre. "The Impressionists," he said thoughtfully, reading from the map. *Maybe. Worth a check.* "They certainly sound boring enough." He stifled a yawn. *What did they do, sit around all day long and try to impress each other? Ha ha.*

His eyes followed his parents, who were heading for the security office. For a moment he considered telling them where he was going, but on the other hand. . . .

Well, I'll have the kids back in five minutes, he promised himself. *They'll never even know I'm gone!*

He grinned and loped toward the Impressionist exhibit.

Jessica frowned. Whatever time it was in Sweet Valley, her parents should be answering the phone. *Don't they know I'm trying to get hold of them?* she asked herself with growing irritation, listening to the phone ring once . . . twice . . . three times. *Don't they even care that Lizzie and I are being pursued by—*

Click. Jessica rolled her eyes. "Hello! My dippy sisters are in France and—" She replaced the receiver.

By now, she'd practically memorized the entire greeting.

Honestly, she thought as she returned to the café, *if I ever hear my dippy brother's voice again, I'll probably scream!*

Scratch the Impressionists, Steven thought, his eyes darting around the map. "Some of those guys were actually pretty cool dudes," he muttered, thinking about the artwork he'd seen. Especially that one guy whose pictures were made up of millions and millions of tiny dots. What was his name? Georges something. *Seurat, that's right. When you looked at the painting up close, it looked like a total mess,* Steven thought, shaking his head. *But from a distance, it was a pretty neat picture!*

Steven cleared his throat and checked his watch. *Hmm. He'd spent just a little more time in that exhibit than he'd planned.*

Steven spread the map in front of him and picked another spot. *No jewelry,* he told himself, running his hand through his hair. *The kids'd like that kind of stuff. No costume rooms— Hey!*

He raised an eyebrow. "Suits of armor," he said, nodding slowly.

Yup, suits of armor would bore my sisters out of their tree!

*   *   *

"You make the call this time," Jessica insisted.

"What makes you think they'll answer now?" Elizabeth asked. She looked around the crowded café. A waitress smiled as she walked by, balancing two heavy plates on each arm. Elizabeth could practically hear Jessica's stomach rumbling.

Jessica let out her breath slowly. "Maybe I'm psychic or something. Go ahead, give it a try."

Elizabeth hesitated. "But every time we make a call from that phone, it costs us a whole lot of money. Even if we just get the answering machine. We don't have much cash left."

Jessica frowned. Then her face brightened. "Tell you what. Call collect!"

"Collect!" A smile spread across Elizabeth's face. "It won't cost us a cent! Jessica, you're a genius."

"I know," Jessica said, fanning herself. "Now, go! Hurry!"

Elizabeth frowned. Jessica seemed awfully anxious all of a sudden. "Do you really have some sixth sense about them answering this time?" Elizabeth asked. "Or are you just trying to get rid of me?"

"Moi?" Jessica opened her eyes very wide. "Why in the world would I want to get rid of you?"

Steven was beginning to get tired. The twins were nowhere to be found. They weren't in the armor exhibit. They weren't in the room with all the funny little sculptures of—

He rounded a corner at full speed and nearly bumped into a security guard. "Sorry," Steven shouted back over his shoulder, forgetting for a moment that he was in France.

The guard scowled and spoke rapidly in French.

"Hey, I said I was sorry!" Turning around, Steven held up his hands and backpedaled. "Umm . . ." *How do you say it in French, anyway?* "I'm hungry" is "J'ai faim"—"I have hunger." So "I'm sorry" would be "I have sorrow"—"J'ai—you know. J'ai sorry," he added helplessly.

The guard widened his eyes and took a step forward.

Steven sighed. *Why don't they all learn to speak English?* he thought irritably. "Listen, I'm sorry, OK? No harm done—j'ai sorry!"

He stopped abruptly. Hanging on the wall above the security guard was a painting that showed a scene in a street café. "The museum café," Steven whispered, his eyes dancing. "Of course!" He kicked himself mentally. How long could the twins stay out of the snack bar?

Turning quickly on his heels, he sped off down the hallway.

Jessica watched eagerly as Elizabeth disappeared into the hallway where the phone was. The moment her sister was gone, Jessica leaped up from her seat and signaled the waitress. "Mademoiselle?" she called out.

The waitress approached the table, a smile on her face. "Yes?" she said in English. "May I help you?"

"Umm, how do you say 'I absolutely must have pastry' in French?" Jessica ventured. Translating was hard enough, even when she wasn't starving to death.

The waitress nodded. "A very useful expression. Yes. *J'ai vraiment besoin d'une pâtisserie.*"

"*J'ai vraiment besoin d'une pâtisserie,*" Jessica echoed. "But—" She hesitated. "Better make it two."

"Yes. One for you and one for your sister." The waitress flashed Jessica a smile and disappeared.

One for me, and one for my sister? Jessica thought with a frown. *More like one for now—and one for later.*

Steven was almost to the door of the café when a whistle blew. Out of nowhere, five uniformed security guards blocked his path.

"Huh?" he said, slowing down quickly and craning his neck over his shoulder to see what the fuss was all about. But to his surprise, the guards grabbed him instead.

"What's going on?" Steven yelled. He felt himself being jerked up off the floor. One especially rough pair of hands started to search through his pockets, and Steven was thrust against the wall.

"Hold still," one of the guards hissed. "Do not try to move, or it will go all ze worse for you."

Huh? Steven choked back a response. *How do you say "I want a lawyer" in French?* He tried to push himself backward—and got an elbow in the ribs for his trouble.

"I said, hold still." Steven felt someone tear open his backpack. Out of the corner of his eye, he could see one college shirt after another being tossed on the floor.

"All this for running in the halls?" Steven wailed. He thought about turning around—but his ribs were sore enough. "Even grade school was never *this* bad!"

"Running in ze halls?" The guard's voice sounded unbelieving. "If it were only running! No, no, young man—you have stolen a valuable item from ze museum!"

"A what?" Steven couldn't help himself. He tried to force his way around so he could stare his accuser in the face. But halfway there he felt a fist land in his stomach. "Oooof!" He doubled over quickly. "I never took anything," he gasped, trying to get his wind back.

"A likely story." The voice was cold and hard.

"A piece of clothing from India. Very valuable. Much money. Give it back."

"But I don't have it!" Steven insisted, clutching his aching stomach. *A piece of clothing from India?*

"But you do!" the guard snapped. "You run madly past a guard as if you is in ze Olympics, and you shout you have ze clothing—"

Steven's mouth felt dry. "But I didn't—"

A crowd had gathered. "Zen vair is ze clothing?" the guard demanded.

"I don't know!" Steven almost shouted. He thought back in a panic. He could vaguely remember a costume exhibit in the room next to the hall where he'd begun to run. *But I didn't even go in there!* he told himself. *Why would I want to look at a bunch of dumb clothes, anyway?*

One by one, his T-shirts piled up on the floor.

*   *   *

Elizabeth held her breath as the phone began to ring. *Answer it, somebody,* she begged silently. Figuring out how to make a collect call from the pay phone had been next to impossible. Her French wasn't very good, and the operator's English was worse.

Two rings . . . three . . . four. Elizabeth's heart sank as the answering machine clicked on. "Hello! My dippy sisters are in France—"

"Pardon, mademoiselle," the operator interrupted.

"Wait! Wait!" Elizabeth tried to argue. If she could just hang on till the greeting was done, maybe she could sneak a couple of words onto the tape. "Someone's there, I know it." She crossed her fingers behind her back.

"Mademoiselle!" The voice was unbelieving.

"Umm, umm, just wait a couple of minutes," Elizabeth burst out. "Deux minutes, s'il vous plait!" She strained to hear the greeting. Would Steven ever stop talking?

"—so if you'd like to leave a message," Steven droned on, "press one if it's for me, press two for my parents, and go jump in the lake if—"

The operator said something Elizabeth didn't quite understand.

What's the French word for "emergency"? Elizabeth felt a sense of panic enveloping her. "Au secours!" she cried into the phone. "Help." *Well, it would just have to do.* "Au secours, s'il vous plait!"

"—and don't call us, we'll call you," she heard Steven saying.

There was a beep—and then there was nothing.

Elizabeth stared wordlessly at the phone in her hand. The operator had hung up on her. Slowly she walked back toward the café.

She stopped outside the entrance. *Quite a crowd,* she thought. *Wonder what's going on.* Pushing closer, she saw several uniformed security guards clustered around a figure facing the wall. An enormous pile of clothing lay to one side. Elizabeth squinted. *T-shirts,* she told herself suddenly. *T-shirts with—yes, college logos on them.* She definitely recognized the purple and gold N.J.U. Sewer Rats emblem on one.

Funny, she thought with a shake of her head, crossing into the café. *I know someone who's got one of those shirts.*

My brother Steven!

"So why did you say you had ze clothing?" The guard stared at Steven, a contemptuous look on his face.

Steven slowly bent down and started loading the T-shirts into his backpack. Every single muscle in his body ached. "I didn't," he said weakly. "I never did have it."

"I know zat now." The guard rolled his eyes. "Forty-three shirts, but no sari."

Sari? Steven's heart skipped a beat. "What did you say?" he asked, trying to remain calm. "Forty-three shirts, but no—"

"Sari," the man repeated impatiently. "Ze robe zat ladies in India wear. Ze museum has a precious example from many centuries ago, and—"

"I never said I had a sari," Steven protested.

Suddenly it all became clear. "I was trying to say that I was sorry—you know, apologize—that was all, only I was trying to say it in French because your guard didn't speak English, and the guy heard me say 'J'ai sorry'—s-o-r-r-y—and he must have thought I was saying 'J'ai sari—s-a-r-i.' *I have the sari,*" he translated in his mind. He sighed heavily. "And *now,* if you don't mind," he said, stuffing the last shirt into his backpack and standing up, "I'm going to go look for my sisters."

The guard shook his head. "Closing time," he said without a trace of a smile. Steven could hear an announcement coming over the public-address system.

"Closing time already?" Steven bit his lip.

"Yes." The guard nodded. Then he grinned and narrowed his eyes.

"Sari," he added slyly.

"Now what?" Jessica asked, a worried tone in her voice. "If the museum is about to close, then—"

"Then we have to leave," Elizabeth said. "I just hope—"

She left the sentence unfinished, but Jessica could easily fill in the rest. *I just hope Madame du Noir isn't waiting for us outside, ready to put us under glass!*

The girls got up from the table and wandered down a few hallways. "Do you think we're being paranoid, Jess?" Elizabeth asked suddenly.

Jessica scratched her head and considered. "No," she said at last. "There were our dreams. There was the picture in the paper." She started ticking things off on her fingers. "There's the way she just always seems to know where we are."

"The missing girls," Elizabeth agreed. They passed the royal bedchamber belonging to Napoléon III, who had once ruled France.

"And the things we heard Madame du Noir say at the airport. And at the Centre Pompidou. *And the bakery,*" Jessica added. She shook her head. "No. We're not paranoid. We're just being sensible."

"OK," Elizabeth agreed. Then she paused. "What's that?"

Jessica strained to hear. *A woman's voice, speaking in broken English—*

"Not again!" she groaned, looking frantically for a place to hide.

Twelve

◇

There's only one thing to do, Elizabeth thought. Lifting the velvet rope that divided the hallway from Napoléon III's bedroom, she slipped beneath it. "Hurry!" she hissed to her sister, mentally asking the Louvre staff to forgive her for trespassing.

"I am!" Jessica ducked under the rope, too. "Now what?"

"Under the bed," Elizabeth hissed. She threw herself full length on the floor and crawled beneath the platform. *People sure were smaller in the olden days,* she thought as she moved to one side to make room for Jessica. The bed seemed awfully tiny. *I just hope we'll both fit!*

"Dust," Jessica groaned, wriggling forward.

"Don't sneeze!" Elizabeth insisted. Jessica was right. The floor under the bed was covered with a thick layer of dust. Elizabeth rolled partway over so her head was to one side. She took a deep breath and tried hard not to cough. *When I get out of here, she promised herself, I'm going to write a letter to the Louvre staff about making sure to vacuum under the beds!*

Just then, a terrifyingly familiar voice made Elizabeth's heart lurch. "It is strange, no?" Madame du Noir asked. "I am sure I see zem over ze corner, but zen all at once zey is gone."

If she comes a step nearer I'll scream, Elizabeth thought, reaching in the darkness for her sister's hand and squeezing it hard.

"Ze rope is swinging," Madame du Noir went on. "Someone is been here, and soon."

Elizabeth held her breath. *Keep going,* she begged silently. *Keep going, keep going.*

"Well," Madame du Noir continued, "I keep looking, yes. Ask anyone. Zey will say Madame du Noir are a pair-son who nev-air give up."

For a moment there was silence. Then slowly, footsteps began to echo down the hallway. Soon they disappeared altogether. In the distance a bell rang. "She's gone," Jessica hissed in Elizabeth's ear.

"I know," Elizabeth whispered, feeling her heartbeat gradually return to normal.

"So why are we whispering?" Jessica whispered back.

"I don't know." Elizabeth didn't know how much longer she could stand the dust and darkness. "Do you think it's safe to go out yet?"

"Probably," Jessica said, not moving.

There was a pause. *It's pretty awful under here,* Elizabeth thought, wondering if there might be large insects living in Napoléon III's mattress. *But what if—* She swallowed hard. *What if Madame du Noir's only tricking us and hasn't really gone anywhere at all? What if she's ready to pounce on us? She said she never gives up.*

"Let's wait a little longer," she whispered to her sister, her throat dry as a bone. "You know. Just in case."

"How do you say 'I'm going to sue you for false arrest' in French?" Steven demanded. He had just spotted his parents coming down the steps of the museum with Madame du Noir. "You're never going to believe what those idiots did! I mean—"

"Steven, what are we going to do with you?" His mother looked exasperated.

Steven's mouth hung open. "What—what do you mean, Mom?"

Mr. Wakefield jumped in. "She means that it's bad enough to lose two kids without losing a third as well."

"Yeah, well, I—"

"I don't care how old you are, you have *got* to stay with us at all times," Mr. Wakefield said sternly.

"But, Dad!" Steven interrupted. "I thought I knew where the girls were, so—"

"You saw them?" Mr. Wakefield raised his eyebrows and stepped toward his son. "In the museum? Where?"

"Well, I didn't exactly *see* them," Steven began.

"Please don't run off again unless you actually do see them," Mr. Wakefield told him firmly. "Understand?"

Steven grimaced and nodded.

"I am much sorry." Madame du Noir joined the conversation. "As I am tell you when we are in ze bedroom of Napoléon III, I am almost certain I am see Zhessica as we turn ze corner. Or pair-haps it was Elizabess. I am much, much sorry." She gave a formal little bow. "Pardon."

Pardon, Steven thought with disgust. *Pardon means sorry. Of course. How incredibly stupid of me. If only I'd said "Pardon," the guards would never have taken off after me, and I'd have checked the café. Where they were probably stuffing their faces with croissants.*

"I know what you mean, Madame." Mrs. Wakefield nodded at Madame du Noir. "For a second or two, when we were in that bedroom exhibit . . ." She paused. "It sounds funny, I know, but I could almost feel the twins. I could almost sense their presence."

"Pair-haps I should not have talked in zat room," Madame du Noir said darkly. "Ze two of you were quiet. Pair-haps if I had not been chitter-ing on and on, you might have could tell exactly where zeir presence was. Or pair-haps . . ." Madame du Noir sighed. "Pair-haps my eye is no more working."

"You've been doing all you can," Mr. Wakefield said kindly. He sighed. "I think we could all use a bite to eat. I saw a café around the corner."

Café, Steven thought bitterly. *I bet they were in the museum café, all right. I bet you anything!*

* * *

"I think the museum is all locked up," Jessica said, dismay creeping into her voice.

Elizabeth blinked as she emerged from under the bed. "It does seem awfully empty," she said, her words echoing in the stillness. "The lights are out, and there's nobody around."

"Well, that's a good thing, anyway." Jessica laughed hollowly and brushed some dust off her sweatshirt. "I'm sure my hair is a total disaster."

"Uh-huh," Elizabeth said absentmindedly. She took a deep breath of almost dust-free air. "Listen, Jessica, did you notice something weird about the way Madame du Noir was talking when she was here?"

"Weird isn't the word I'd use." Jessica looked up. "Scary is more like it. The way she said 'I will never give up until I have caught those two'!"

"That's what she said?" Elizabeth wrinkled her brow. Somehow she couldn't remember those exact words.

"Well, she said it in a scarier voice," Jessica admitted. "Like this." She put on a witch's cackle and spoke: "I—ha ha!—will never—"

"Oh, she did not either," Elizabeth interrupted, managing a faint grin. "No, what I thought was kind of weird was that she was talking in English."

Jessica raised her eyebrows. "Hey, you're right! She was."

"And I heard more than one pair of footsteps," Elizabeth went on. "Did you?"

Jessica considered for a moment, then nodded. "So someone was with her."

"Someone who speaks English," Elizabeth added. "Someone who knows she's looking for us. Someone who—" She hated to say it. "She might have a, what do you call it, an accomplice. Like in the Amanda Howard books. You know, the criminals always have someone working with them—"

"Oh, man," Jessica said slowly. "Oh, man."

They stared at each other.

"Well, there's nothing we can do about it right now," Elizabeth said at last. "As they say in French, 'Nous ne sommes pas encore mortes.'"

"Huh?" Jessica said.

"It means, 'We're not dead yet,'" Elizabeth translated. *Thank you,* Speak French Just as a Native Might Do! "Now what do we do till the museum opens?"

"That's easy," Jessica said. She pointed to Napoléon III's bed. "I suggest we sleep like queens tonight," she said grandly. "In the royal bed."

Elizabeth couldn't help but grin. "All right." As she climbed onto the bed, the mattress squeaked. "On one condition."

"What's that?" Jessica asked.

"We draw the draperies." Elizabeth pulled the curtains that surrounded the bed. They billowed down, completely hiding the girls from sight.

"To protect us from Madame du Noir?" Jessica asked.

Elizabeth shook her head. "To protect us from janitors and security guards!"

Now this, Steven thought with satisfaction the next morning. *This is totally decent!*

He settled back into his seat on the Metro subway car and grinned. One station after another flashed past, but the train was so smooth, Steven hardly noticed the stops and starts. "This ride is unbelievable," he muttered, closing his eyes and listening to the doors of the car open and shut. *Wouldn't it be awesome to have something like this in L.A.? Maybe they could build a subway between—*

Well, between his house and school might be a good place to begin.

"Steven!" Mrs. Wakefield poked him. He jerked his eyes open. "Look for the girls, would you please?"

"Sorry," Steven murmured. *That's right,* he reminded himself, *we're down here looking for the twins.* Madame du Noir had suggested that they spend a few hours crisscrossing Paris by subway. "Ze stations are warm and dry, and no one will bother zem," she had said. "Pair-haps zey are hiding in a Metro station."

Well, pair-haps zey were. Steven squashed his nose flat against the window of the train and stared hopefully through the glass.

"I'm sorry," Jessica said later that same morning, "but it's no wonder Napoléon III was such a bad emperor. If I had to sleep on that bed every night, I'd be cranky all the time, too."

Elizabeth settled back against the park bench they were sitting on. "I know what you mean."

"Talk about a hard mattress!" Jessica continued. "I don't think I slept a wink all night long."

"Oh, you did too." Elizabeth frowned. "You

were snoring so loudly I was afraid they'd find us."

"I was not!" Jessica glared at her sister.

"Yes, you were," Elizabeth insisted. "It's a good thing we don't have to share a room at home."

Jessica rolled her eyes. "Well, *if* I snored—*which* I didn't—it was only because of the dust under the bed. I'm allergic to dust, in case you've forgotten. And it was your idea to hide under the bed in the first place."

"Would you rather be put under glass?" Elizabeth asked harshly.

Jessica bit her lip. "Well—"

"Bonjour, bonjour!" An elderly lady with shoulder-length gray hair approached, tossing peanuts to a group of squirrels nearby. She spoke to them rapidly in French and held out a handful of nuts.

"Umm, merci," Jessica murmured, taking the nuts and scattering them at her feet.

The woman smiled broadly. "Ah!" she said in an unusually high-pitched voice. "You are not Frenchlings!"

Jessica suppressed a smile. "We're American."

"America! America!" The woman seemed so delighted, Jessica thought she was about to pull an American flag out of her pocket and start waving it around. "I loo-oove America!" She sat on the bench right between the girls.

Jessica moved over a little to make room. The woman was wearing a black dress that reminded her of Madame du Noir's. *Must be the little-old-lady uniform here in France,* she thought. Her hair was beautifully styled. In fact, she was one of the most elegant old women Jessica had ever seen. The only thing that spoiled the picture was a few faint hairs on the old lady's upper lip.

This woman also wore a scarf, Jessica noticed, but her scarf was dark blue with pink dots, not black-and-white as Madame du Noir's had been.

"America!" the woman said enthusiastically. Jessica watched her lips carefully. It was hard to understand her accent.

"New Yorick?" the woman asked. Jessica frowned. "Shee-cago, bang bang?" The old lady made a gun with her forefinger and thumb and pointed it, grinning, at Elizabeth. "Teck-sas?"

Oh, I get it, Jessica thought. *She wants to know where we're from.* "We live in Sweet Valley, California," she said loudly in the old woman's ear.

"Califor-nee!" The woman seemed so thrilled, Jessica thought she might have a heart attack right there. "Ell Ay, Holly-wood!"

"Near there," Jessica admitted, grinning. She kind of liked this silly old lady. And it was nice to meet someone who was so friendly.

"Ah, and your names?" The woman stood up and leaned toward Jessica.

Jessica hesitated, but only for a moment. "I'm Jessica Wakefield," she said, reaching to shake the old woman's hand.

"Zhes-see-ca." The woman smiled broadly and rolled the name around on her tongue.

Elizabeth stood up and smiled politely. "And I'm Elizabeth."

"Ay-lee-sa-bess." The woman began to bow.

Halfway down she changed the bow into a curtsy. "Enchantée."

"Enchantée," Jessica repeated. "And you are—"

The woman started to speak, then swallowed hard. "Madame Renault," she said at last. "Enchantée."

"Enchantée," the girls echoed her.

"I—" Madame Renault seemed to be groping for words. "I very lonely old lady. Husband die, cheeldren—" She moved her hand as if it were climbing a staircase.

"Children all grown up," Jessica supplied, her eyes twinkling. She liked this kind of conversation.

"Yes!" Madame Renault nodded furiously. "Cheeldren all grow up. I so, so lonely."

"Don't they ever come to visit?" Elizabeth asked with concern, leaning closer to Madame Renault.

"Zey—" Madame Renault shrugged. "Live far, far gone. Shee-cago, bang bang," she added quickly. "And Teck-sas."

"That is pretty far," Jessica agreed, her heart going out to this poor lonely widow whose children couldn't come to visit. "How about your friends?"

"Old people all dorky," Madame Renault replied.

Jessica held back a snicker. Dorky? Where had she heard a word like that?

Madame Renault smiled again. "Voulez-vous you girls—come wiss me—my apartment?" She made elaborate hand signals. "You join me in cup of tea, yes?"

Jessica giggled. A picture rose into her mind: Madame Renault in a bathing suit, paddling around the edge of an enormous teacup. "We'd love to," she said.

"Of course," Elizabeth agreed.

"Oh, good, good, good!" Madame Renault wrung her hands together. "Let's party! We go Metro, yes?" She darted toward the entrance of the park.

"You think it's OK?" Elizabeth asked Jessica doubtfully, standing up.

"Of course it's OK," Jessica assured her. "She's really nice." She grinned mischievously. "Besides, we could use a free cup of something."

"All right." Elizabeth began to follow. "And anyway, *most* old ladies are the safest people on earth."

Jessica thought of Madame du Noir and shuddered. "Yup," she agreed, watching Madame Renault's blue-and-pink scarf flapping up ahead. "The safest people on earth."

Thirteen

Rush hour was over, and Steven stretched out across two subway seats. *This really is the life,* he thought happily, glancing around the almost empty train. "How much longer, Mom?" he called down to his mother, who was riding with Mr. Wakefield in the back of the car.

Madame du Noir, sitting across from Steven, answered first. "Zere are zhust a few more stations I zink we should see. Zen—" She spread out her arms. "If zey are not zere, we will zink of somezing else."

Like checking the café in the Louvre, Steven thought, rolling his eyes. The train slowed down, and the lights of the next station came into view.

"The only good thing is that they've been missing forty-eight hours now," Steven could hear his mother saying. "Now the police should start looking, too."

"Keep your eye apart," Madame du Noir advised Steven as the train pulled to a stop. "Zis station is big. Many trains stop, and zere are many shoplets."

Shoplets? Steven thought. The doors slid open, but no one got on. His eyes scanned the faces on the platform. *Oh, right. Droplets are little drops, so shoplets would be—*

Suddenly Steven sat bolt upright. Two blond heads were clearly visible down at the other end of the platform—about to board a train heading in the opposite direction! "The twins!" he shouted, springing to his feet and dashing for the door.

Madame du Noir gasped and jumped out of her seat, too. Steven grabbed her arm and lunged for the doorway. The empty space in front of him was narrowing quickly. "Let me out! Open the doors!" he yelled, though he knew the motorman couldn't possibly hear him.

There was only one thing to do. Diving like a basketball player after a loose ball, Steven tumbled through the door and out onto the platform, Madame du Noir beside him, just as the train began to pull out of the station. Out of the corner of his eye, Steven could see his parents through the window, waving and shouting until the train disappeared.

Man, that was close! Steven thought, trying to catch his breath. "You all right, Madame?"

But Madame du Noir was already on her feet and running down the platform toward the twins. "Zhessica!" she shouted, waving her arms. "Elizabess!"

Quickly, Steven picked himself up and ran after

her on the platform. The girls' train didn't seem all that far away. He could see them standing there, right by the open doors. Steven waved desperately, hoping to attract the girls' attention. *I hope it isn't too late,* he thought, his breath coming in gasps. *I hope it isn't—*

The doors closed with an ominous hiss.

—too late, Steven finished with a sense of dread.

"Stop, stop!" he yelled. Little by little, the train began to move.

"Oh, man." Steven felt like crying. The train was so close, he could almost reach out and touch it. *But it might as well be a million miles away.* The train started to pick up speed. The gentle sound of the engine filled the quiet subway station.

Steven bit his tongue, watching his sisters take a seat in the train. They were facing away from him, in earnest conversation with a gray-haired old woman. Steven frowned. Why would his sisters run like crazy from one old woman just to hang out with another?

"I like this apartment," Elizabeth said. The girls were sitting in Madame Renault's dining room, sipping the tea she'd made for them. Madame Renault was in the kitchen.

"Me too," Jessica agreed, setting down her teacup. "Small, but nice."

She studied the room. Madame Renault lived in a first-floor apartment with a large plate-glass window that looked out onto the street. The dining room shelves were covered with knickknacks, and the friendly smell of boiling tea filled the whole place.

Madame Renault bustled into the dining room, holding a package of cookies. "You like?" she asked shyly, holding the package out.

"Umm, merci beaucoup," Jessica said, taking four.

Madame Renault laughed—a low laugh at first, suddenly becoming more and more high-pitched. "You like ver' much!" she said.

Jessica smiled. "Mmm hmm!" she said, about to take a big bite. Then she considered that might not be the polite, mature thing to do. "I mean, yes, very much."

Madame Renault offered the package to Elizabeth, who took just one. "Where you like go next?" she asked, staring hard at the twins.

"Maybe the Eiffel Tower," Elizabeth answered. "I've always wanted to see that." She took another sip of tea.

"Ah! Ze Tower! Awesome!" Madame Renault screwed up her eyes and clenched her fists together with delight.

Jessica popped a cookie in her mouth to keep herself from laughing. For someone who didn't speak much English, Madame Renault sure knew a lot of American slang expressions. *She's probably spent a lot of time around American teenagers,* Jessica thought. *She's definitely friendly enough!*

Madame Renault beamed at the twins. "I many times go to Eiffel Tower. My family go—when I am little—" She swallowed. "When I am little girly."

Jessica tried to imagine Madame Renault as a little girl, but she couldn't. She was so old and gray and . . . Jessica peered closely at Madame Renault's face. It looked like she'd grown a few whiskers.

Jessica glanced down at her teacup, not wanting Madame Renault to notice she'd been staring. "Umm . . . could I have some more tea?"

"*Mais oui!*" Madame Renault scurried back to the kitchen.

Jessica grinned. She knew that one from French class: "But of course!"

She turned toward her sister. "Hey, Lizzie! Did you see Madame Renault's little mustache?"

Elizabeth looked at her sternly. "Don't you know that old ladies sometimes grow whiskers?" she hissed back. "Be polite!"

"Sheesh, who's not being polite?" Jessica asked, cramming another cookie into her mouth. "I was just saying, that's all."

Great. Just great.

Steven scuffed his shoe against the concrete floor of the subway platform. His parents were on a train going one way, and his sisters were on another train going another way, and he was here with Madame du Noir in the middle of a subway station in the middle of a city he'd never been to before, and—

Madame du Noir laid a hand on his shoulder. "Grin up," she said gently. "You tried your best, zat is what counts."

Steven shrugged and stared at the platform. "Yeah, whatever." *If only I'd noticed them sooner,* he thought with a frown. *If only I'd run a little faster. If only—*

"Come." Madame du Noir steered him toward the stairs. Together they walked up a flight, then up another. "I show you ze way back to your hotel," she explained, making a sudden left turn and walking up onto the sidewalk. "We wait zere for your parent."

"My parents," Steven corrected her, but Madame du Noir didn't seem to notice. "I am remember one time when I am young girl," she went on, taking Steven's arm and steering him across a busy intersection.

"What happened?" Steven asked curiously.

"I am playing outside my house," Madame du Noir told him. "Zen suddenly I am see my mother get on a bus in front of me. I am think, 'My mother am leaving town!'"

"That must have been a little scary," Steven said sympathetically.

"I cry, I run to bus dri-vair," Madame du Noir said. "I am say, 'Stop ze bus! My mama must come back to me!' Dri-vair cannot hear me, so I run into ze street."

"Here?" Steven stared openmouthed at the roaring traffic all around him.

"Oh, yes," Madame du Noir assured him. "Dri-vair stop. I tell him what is ze problem, and we look on ze bus." She spread her hands out wide. "My mama is not on ze bus after all. It was zhust a woman who look like her."

Steven shook his head. "Nice try, Madame, but I'm sure it was the twins."

Madame du Noir nodded. "Well, pair-haps you are right."

Steven jumped as he heard a squealing of brakes. A horn honked directly behind him. A battered old car that had once been blue pulled up onto the sidewalk, and the driver waved furiously. For a moment Steven wondered if he was about to be kidnapped. Then he breathed a sigh of relief. *It's only that crazy baker, Monsieur What's-his-name,* he thought.

"Voilà, my really cool car!" Monsieur Courbet announced. He swung open the doors. "Zhump in!"

"Ze wedding are over," Monsieur Courbet explained a few moments later, guiding his car through the streets of Paris at what seemed to Steven like a hundred miles an hour. "You may eat what you please!"

His lips white with fear, Steven stared hungrily at the pastries beside him in the backseat. They looked delicious, but something told him he shouldn't let go of the seat back long enough to pick one up.

Monsieur Courbet took a sudden left turn, but most of Steven's insides continued straight ahead. "Oof," he groaned. Then the car accelerated quickly until it was about two inches behind a police van. Monsieur Courbet happily stomped on the brakes, nearly sending himself flying through the windshield.

"A big strong boy like you need much pastry!" he shouted, throwing the car into a different gear and snaking in and out of traffic. "Eat!" Steven looked once more at the pastries and made up his mind. *Better to die on a full stomach than on an empty one!* Cautiously, he let go of the seat back and snared a slice of cake.

The car skidded to a stop at a traffic light. "Red," Monsieur Courbet said gloomily, drumming his fingers rhythmically against the steering wheel. "Zey are always red in zis neighborhood—ze Bastille."

"Or maybe they're not red enough of the time," Steven muttered, taking a bite of cake. He stared out the window. *Nice old neighborhood,* he thought. *Fancy houses, big windows, green trees—*

Steven gasped. The building ahead of him had a huge window—and through the glass, Steven saw two figures sitting at a table. Two very familiar figures.

As Monsieur Courbet pressed down on the gas pedal, Steven sat up straight. "Stop the car!" he yelled.

"Right away, sir!" Monsieur Courbet saluted and jammed on the brakes.

"Hey!" The cake flew across the backseat, and Steven clutched his stomach. "Thanks, but . . . uh . . . maybe not quite so fast next time, OK?" he requested weakly.

Dingdong!

"Do you say 'dingdong' in French?" Elizabeth asked, listening to the doorbell chime. She frowned as the bell pealed again—and again. Three times in all.

"Sheesh, talk about impatient!" Jessica giggled. "You'd think it was Steven or somebody!"

Dingdooong! A scowl creased Madame Renault's face. Muttering something under her breath, she strode quickly to the entrance to the apartment. For the first time, Elizabeth noticed that the door was triple-locked. *This didn't look like a high-crime area,* she thought with surprise. *But I guess you never really know these days.*

Madame Renault unfastened one lock. "I'm coming, I'm coming!" she yelled in French. Elizabeth couldn't help noticing how powerfully built Madame Renault seemed to be for a little old lady. She fumbled with the second lock.

Dingdong!

Madame Renault took a quick glance over her shoulder at the twins. Click!

As Madame Renault turned the second lock, Elizabeth could hear someone speaking on the other side of the door.

"I must have Zhessica—"

Elizabeth felt her blood run cold. She'd know that voice anywhere. Grabbing Jessica's hand, she sprinted toward the back of the apartment.

Fourteen

Just when we've found a friend, Jessica thought, panic rising in her throat. Whirling around while Elizabeth dragged her toward the back of the apartment, she caught sight of Madame Renault struggling with the last lock. "What about our bags?" she hissed to her sister, fighting to stay in control.

"Forget the bags!" Elizabeth replied through gritted teeth.

Ahead of them was an open window. "You first," Jessica whispered, helping Elizabeth climb through it. *Good thing we're on the first floor*, she thought, preparing to follow her sister. It was a tight squeeze. *Too bad we didn't get to say good-bye to Madame Renault, but when a mass murderer's on your trail . . .*

"Oooof!" Hitting the sidewalk harder than she'd expected, Jessica felt her knee give way.

"Can you walk?" Elizabeth helped her up.

"Umm, yeah." Jessica tested the knee. "I guess

we'd better find a phone and call home," she mumbled, limping down the sidewalk as fast as she could. "I don't care what time it is there, I don't care if we get the machine, we've got to let them know about this. We've—"

"We were keeping all the money we had left in our backpacks," Elizabeth broke in bleakly. "And our backpacks—"

"Are back in Madame Renault's apartment," Jessica finished, shaking her head. "Where we can't go because Madame du Noir is about to break the door down. Great. Just great. We'll have to make another collect call."

"We've got to go to the police now," Elizabeth said. Jessica could hear an edge to her voice. "We've got to, Jess."

"No way!" Jessica's lips curled apart. "It would be so easy for Madame du Noir to find us, Lizzie. Wouldn't you bet she's been in touch with the police already? They'd probably call her right away, thinking they were handing us over to some safe little old lady. Ha!"

"You're probably right." Elizabeth spoke softly. They stared at each other.

"So where's the nearest phone?" Jessica asked bitterly.

Dingdooong!

"This is crazy," Steven muttered, removing his hand from Madame Renault's doorbell. "What's this woman got—forty-two locks or something?"

"*Ouvrez la porte, s'il vous plaît!*" Madame du Noir

rapped on the door with her knuckles and spoke in a firm voice.

The woman on the other side of the door mumbled something.

"*Maintenant!*" Madame du Noir ordered. Turning to Steven, she whispered, "That mean 'right now.'"

Steven couldn't stand it any longer. "Be right back," he whispered to Madame du Noir. *I'll get their attention through the window,* he thought, dashing out onto the sidewalk.

He ran to the side of the house and looked through the window. He began to wave his arms to get the twins' attention when he realized the twins weren't where they'd been sitting a moment ago. Rubbing his eyes, he looked through the glass again. The room was totally empty.

"Everyzing all right?" Monsieur Courbet leaned out of the window of his old car, which was blocking traffic on the street.

"No." Steven shook his head. "I can't see them. They must be farther back in the apartment or something. And the old lady inside is taking years to open up the stupid door."

Monsieur Courbet frowned. "I will go fetch ze police," he said, shutting off the motor and hopping onto the sidewalk.

Steven didn't wait. Setting his jaw, he darted back inside the apartment building.

"She say she have no girls inside," Madame du Noir reported to Steven as soon as he arrived by her side. They stood in the doorway of the apartment, facing a gray old woman with a faint mustache. She wore a black dress and a blue scarf dotted with pink.

Steven's eyes flashed. "I *saw* them. They were there, plain as day!" He wished this other old lady could speak English like Madame du Noir. The two women had been having a shouting match in French ever since the door had opened, and by now Steven's head was spinning with the strange words. "I saw them myself," he told the other woman slowly, pointing to his chest and his eyes. "I'm not lying!"

The old woman shouted something in French. She motioned to the door.

Frustrated, Steven turned to Madame du Noir. "Monsieur Courbet went to get the police."

Madame du Noir nodded. "Zen we wait for the gendarmerie—the police." She stuck her foot in the doorway.

"*Gendarmerie!*" The old woman spat out the word. Throwing herself against the door, she tried to knock Madame du Noir's foot out of the way. "*Non! Non! Non!*"

Madame du Noir moaned as the door caught squarely on her heel. Jumping forward quickly, Steven held the door ajar with his shoulder. *Wow, she's strong for an old lady,* he thought. "If you don't have anything to hide, why are you so worried about the police?" Steven shouted.

The only answer was a muffled growl. Running footsteps sounded behind Steven. "We are here," Monsieur Courbet panted. Two uniformed men dashed by Steven and through the open door. *The police!* Steven thought gratefully. Letting go of the door, he rubbed his shoulder muscles. *What a workout!*

The police officers spoke rapidly to the woman. "Her name is Madame Renault," Madame du Noir translated for Steven. "She say she nev-air hear of two twin girls such as your sisters."

Steven thought he'd never been so aggravated in his life. "But I saw——"

Madame du Noir put a firm hand on his arm. "Ze police will do zeir job, just wait."

Wait? Steven thought bleakly. *How am I supposed to just wait when my sisters keep appearing and then vanishing into nowhere?*

But there didn't seem to be any other choice.

"There is no way we're going back to Madame Renault's anytime soon." Elizabeth spoke firmly. "Money or no money, it's just too dangerous."

"I—I guess you're right." Jessica didn't like to admit it. Already she felt dangerously close to starvation. *How long can you live without buying food, anyway?*

"I wish Mom and Dad would come home from wherever they are," Elizabeth said, shaking her head. "Collect calls just don't work out if no one's home." She spoke lightly, but Jessica could hear the tension in her sister's voice. "I mean, if *you* can't convince the operator to say a few words onto the tape, *no one can.*"

"Thanks, I think." Jessica thought back to her argument with the operator a few minutes ago. She'd done her best, but Steven's stupid message had just gone on and on. "Next time we travel, we need one of those phone cards."

"Yeah." Elizabeth nodded. They turned a corner near a small sidewalk café. Jessica could almost taste the soups and salads. She resolved not to think about chocolate éclairs.

"So if we don't go to Madame Renault's," Jessica began, doing her best to ignore a little boy eating an ice cream cone nearby, "where should we go?" Elizabeth considered. "To the Eiffel Tower," she said at last.

"Bo-ring," Jessica muttered. "What's so great about a humongous TV antenna, anyway?"

"I've always wanted to see it," Elizabeth said reproachfully. "And besides, I told Madame Renault that might be our next stop. If we're lucky, she might come and find us."

Slowly Jessica grinned. "With our bags," she added.

"And we could have our own private little memorial service there, too," Elizabeth said quietly as they walked on.

"Memorial service?" Jessica's eyes flew open wide. "For us?"

"No, silly." But Elizabeth didn't smile. "For the girls who couldn't escape the evil clutches of Madame du Noir."

"Good idea," Jessica agreed. She reached for her sister's hand. T'amuses-toi bien? she asked herself, remembering how Katharine had translated "Are you having fun?" on the plane.

She shook her head violently.

Mais non!

She wasn't *amuses-toi bien*-ing at all!

"No sign of them?" Steven stared in amazement at Madame du Noir, and then at the police officers.

"No girls anywhere in ze apartment." Madame du Noir patted his hand. "I am sor-ry. Pair-haps you are mees-taken."

Steven slumped against the wall. *The third time,* he thought bitterly. *Three times now, I've seen my sisters—and I just can't hang on!*

"Come." Madame du Noir took him by the arm and led him out of the apartment building. Behind them, a door slammed. *Madame Renault is one weird customer,* Steven thought. He slid back into Monsieur Courbet's car and jerked the rear door closed behind him.

"No twins?" Monsieur Courbet asked in surprise from the driver's seat.

"Here today, gone tomorrow," Steven grumbled, tracing a design on the window of the car. "Now you see them, now you don't. Poof!" He snapped his fingers. "I don't get it. They vanish, just like that."

"Zat woman was hiding somezing," Madame du Noir said with conviction.

"Many sorries," Monsieur Courbet told Steven. Starting the engine, he pulled out into a tiny break in the traffic. Almost immediately there was a loud honking behind the little car.

"*Gendarmerie,*" Madame du Noir said hastily, leaning across to Monsieur Courbet.

"What could ze police possible want wiss me?" Monsieur Courbet pulled the car to a halt across two lanes of traffic.

Oh, plenty of things, Steven thought, watching one of the officers approach the car. *Reckless driving, failure to signal turns, parking in the middle of traffic, driving on the sidewalk, to name a few.*

The policeman bent down and spoke rapidly to Monsieur Courbet. Steven could make out a piece of paper in the officer's hand. Monsieur Courbet turned pale.

"What is it?" Steven's heart began to pound furiously. He leaned forward in his seat. "Is it about the twins?"

The officer was speaking again. "Elles ne sont pas encore mortes."

Steven's eyes grew wide with shock. He recognized that expression from *Speak French Just as a Native Might Do!* "They are not dead yet," he translated slowly. "Who's not dead yet?"

"Oh, zis is terrible," Madame du Noir said weakly. She turned back to face Steven. "Zat woman—Madame Renault?"

"Yes," Steven said, feeling his fingers tensing into a fist.

"Ze police, he zink he know her face," Madame du Noir went on, her eyes boring into Steven's. "So he look in photos, and—she is woman who is kidnap American girls in Paris."

"No!" Steven sat straight up, a terrible pounding

in his brain. *My sisters—* "It can't be."

"But it is." Madame du Noir spoke softly. "He say, 'If we have luck, your sisters is not dead yet.'"

Monsieur Courbet rammed the car back into gear. "He go now to radio for upback."

"Backup," Steven said absently. *Man, oh, man!* A million thoughts whirled around in his mind. *Will I ever see the twins again?*

What can I do to save them?
And, most horrible of all:
What on earth am I going to say to Mom and Dad?

Fifteen

With a sigh of relief, Jessica stepped onto the observation platform at the top of the Eiffel Tower. "I think we made it," she whispered to Elizabeth.

"I hope you're right," Elizabeth whispered back. The girls had snuck onto the elevator without paying. Jessica's eyes scanned the crowd at the top, hoping that no one had noticed.

"Uh-oh." Elizabeth pointed to a uniformed policeman who was slowly approaching them.

"Pretend you don't see him," Jessica advised.

But it was too late. "Mademoiselle!" the policeman called to her.

Oops. "Me?" Jessica asked innocently.

The officer came closer. "Ah, you speak English. Your ticket, please."

"Ticket?" Jessica opened her eyes as wide as possible. "What are you talking about, sir?"

"I knew it wouldn't work." Elizabeth looked sadly at the ground.

"Shh!" Jessica took a deep breath. She decided to pretend she hadn't seen the sign downstairs. "Was I supposed to buy a ticket, officer?"

"You need tickets to ride ze elevator," the policeman told her without smiling. "If you have no tickets, zen you must pay now."

"Oh." Jessica's mind raced. *I could pretend my purse was suddenly stolen,* she thought. *Or I could say that the cashier said we didn't have to pay. Or—*

The policeman stared hard at the girls. "One moment," he said slowly. Pulling a piece of paper out of his pocket, he studied it intently. Now he was grinning.

"You're not putting us in jail, are you?" Jessica's heart was beating furiously.

"Jail? No, no!" The policeman seemed amused. "You are ze Misses Oo-ake-feel, are you not?" he asked.

Jessica frowned. Were she and Elizabeth famous or something? "Umm . . . yes," she said hesitantly.

"Twins," the policeman mused. "You have been reported, what you say, lost."

"Missing," Jessica corrected him. She threw an anxious glance at her sister. *Missing!* This was *not* a good sign. "Who reported us?" she asked, bracing herself for the answer.

The policeman consulted the piece of paper again. "Your guardian here in France," he said happily. "Madame du Noir."

Eyes wide with fear, Jessica stared at her sister.

"There's got to be some way out," Elizabeth whispered anxiously.

Jessica's mind darted this way and that. "I don't know how!" she hissed back. "We're about to be—"

She swallowed hard.

"We're about to be thrown into the arms of a serial killer!"

"Zhey are going to break down ze door," Madame du Noir remarked.

Steven felt his muscles tense. Madame Renault had not opened up, even after five minutes of knocking by the police officers.

"Is she still in there?" Steven asked, watching the officers bang at the door with a heavy hammer.

Madame du Noir shrugged. "Where else may she be?"

The policeman's words still echoed in Steven's brain. *Elles ne sont pas encore mortes—they are not dead yet.* He shook his head, but he couldn't shake away the horrible phrase.

The hammers banged into the door with heavy thuds. A few neighbors gathered to watch.

Though it wasn't a cold day, Steven found himself shivering. The thumping of the officers' hammers seemed to match the thumping of his heart. Worse still, he was picturing the hammers in Madame Renault's hand, coming down violently against the heads of—

Don't think about it, Steven commanded himself.

"I'm going outside," he said, bolting through the door into the fresh air.

From where he stood on the sidewalk, the sound of the hammering was muffled. He could almost pretend it was a perfectly ordinary street corner on a perfectly ordinary day. He could see a fish market, a drugstore, a few old apartment buildings, and—

Steven shaded his eyes from the bright light of the lowering sun. *And a woman climbing out of a first-floor window!*

"She's escaping!" he cried as he watched Madame Renault leap into a car, gun the engine, and take off down the street in a cloud of smoke.

"They're safe?"

Mrs. Wakefield could hardly keep the joy out of her voice. Her husband stood nearby in their hotel room, listening intently to her end of the phone conversation.

"Yes . . . yes . . ." Mrs. Wakefield couldn't remember a time when she'd been so happy. "The Eiffel Tower, then. We'll be right there." She hung up the phone and embraced her husband. "Oh, Ned. I was so worried. Let's go down and get a cab."

"Forget a cab." Mr. Wakefield looked at his watch. "I can drive us there faster than any cab-driver. I bet I can rent a car downstairs at the front desk." He strode out the door. "How did they know to get hold of us, anyway? I mean, Madame du Noir's the one who reported them missing, and we don't even know where she is. Or Steven," he added meaningfully.

"Madame du Noir's answering machine," Mrs. Wakefield told him. "She said she'd record a message telling where we could be reached." She followed her husband out the door. "Thank goodness for answering machines!"

"Thank goodness for answering machines," Jessica said sarcastically. She held the phone up to her ear as the machine clicked.

"Hello! My dippy sisters are in France——"

"We know that already!" Jessica slammed down the receiver. Her shoulders slumped forward. "Now what, Lizzie?"

Elizabeth shook her head helplessly.

"Well, we can't stay here, that's for sure." Running her hand through her messy hair, Jessica looked around the platform. They had managed to charm the policeman into giving them a few francs to operate the telescopes so they could get a better view of Paris. As soon as his back was turned, they'd rushed over to the telephones and dropped in one coin after another. No time to mess with another collect call.

And what had they gotten? The answering machine.

Jessica shook her head. *If I ever get home,* she promised herself, *I'm throwing the stupid answering machine out the window!*

"All right." Jessica made up her mind. "Down the stairs."

Elizabeth bit her lip. "What if the policeman sees us?"

"Then he sees us. I'm not being roasted under glass by Madame du Noir!" Jessica straightened up and made a dash for the top of the long, long flight of steps that led to the street.

"Wait for me!" Elizabeth called after her.

Jessica could hear Elizabeth's footsteps behind her, and then she heard other, heavier footsteps, too.

"Stop!" the policeman yelled as she started down the stairs.

"Left," Steven directed, peering anxiously out the side window of Monsieur Courbet's car. Far in front of him he could dimly make out the shape of Madame Renault's car as it weaved in and out of traffic.

"Left?" Monsieur Courbet glanced at Steven.

"Right," Steven replied. Monsieur Courbet nodded and swung the wheel heavily to the right. The jolt threw Steven against the window. "I meant left!" he cried. *Darn it, English could be so confusing.* "You know—umm, *gauche!*"

"Gauche." Monsieur Courbet shrugged and steered the old car to the left, narrowly missing three pedestrians and a school bus. Steven shut his eyes, but quickly snapped them open again. He had to keep Madame Renault in sight no matter what.

From the passenger seat, Madame du Noir spoke up. "She head for ze Eiffel Tower," she said.

Monsieur Courbet's car leaped forward. Steven could see the huge tower looming in front of them.

Seems kind of a weird time for Madame Renault to visit the Eiffel Tower, he thought, *but, hey.*

*   *   *

Mrs. Wakefield shaded her eyes. "I can see it. Turn right."

"I can't!" Mr. Wakefield tried to drift into the next lane, but was driven back by a huge semitrailer. The trucker honked loudly as he barreled on by.

Mrs. Wakefield shook her head. "I knew we should have taken a cab."

"I *know* how to get us there." Mr. Wakefield tried once more to merge right. This time a red Porsche zoomed in front of the rental car without signaling. Honking his horn, Mr. Wakefield swung the wheel back to the left.

Mrs. Wakefield gritted her teeth and stared out at the Eiffel Tower in the late afternoon sun. "This is, what, the fifth time we've gone around this traffic circle?" she asked, the tension rising in her voice.

"Only the fourth." Mr. Wakefield craned his neck. "Let's see—I think I can make it now—there's a spot—"

Mrs. Wakefield held her breath.

"Where did that cement mixer come from, anyway?" Mr. Wakefield growled a moment later. Mrs. Wakefield clutched the door handle without saying a word.

"He's going to catch up," Elizabeth gasped. She took a terrified glance back at the police officer, who was coming down the steps two at a time. She tried to quicken her pace.

"Hurry!" Jessica commanded breathlessly.

"I am!" In another moment, Elizabeth guessed,

the policeman would be close enough to touch them. He would grab her shirt collar, and then march them back upstairs and call Madame du Noir.

They sped around a landing and down the next flight. "Keep going!" Jessica panted. "We're getting there!"

Whatever happens, I won't go with Madame du Noir quietly, Elizabeth promised herself. Ahead of her, she saw Jessica dash through a heavy fire door and stop abruptly. Elizabeth didn't have time to ask questions. She sailed through the door, her legs churning like an eggbeater, and turned—

In time to see Jessica slam the door firmly in the policeman's face!

"Oh, my gosh," Elizabeth whispered. The officer fell to the ground, muttered something in French, and closed his eyes. She turned to her sister, eyes wide with fright. "You've killed him!"

"No way." Jessica's voice was steely hard. "I just knocked him out, is all." Moving closer, Elizabeth could see that the officer was still breathing. "And before you get all moral on me," Jessica continued, putting her hands on her hips, "let me remind you that he was going to return us to the care of an ax murderer."

"OK, OK." Elizabeth's palms felt sweaty. "I'll worry about it later. If we ever get out of this mess, that is."

"We're getting close now." Jessica ran down, down, down, Elizabeth at her heels. "One more fire door and—"

But as Jessica pulled open the last fire door, she gasped.

Elizabeth followed her gaze. There, standing at the very bottom of the staircase, was Madame du Noir.

"Aha! Ze twins!" Madame du Noir shouted, pointing an accusing finger in their direction.

Sixteen

◇

Unbelieving, Jessica stared at Madame du Noir. It seemed that the old lady's face curled up into a wicked grin.

Jessica turned toward her sister, knowing there was only one solution. "Up!" Jessica commanded, slamming the heavy fire door against Madame du Noir.

The girls flew back up the stairs as fast as they could, stepping carefully over the unconscious policeman. "What will we do—when we—get back to the top?" Elizabeth panted as they ran.

Jessica shrugged. "We'll figure that out—when we get there." She gasped for breath. Already her side was aching. But she couldn't stop. *We've got to get away,* she thought. *We've got to!*

"What did you say?" Steven came running up to Madame du Noir. Ahead of him stretched a long line of tourists waiting to get into the elevator. "Did you see Madame Renault?"

Madame du Noir clutched Steven's arm. "No, no, not Madame Renault. It was your sis-tairs!" She pointed vaguely in the direction of the stairs. "Zey were coming downstairs—but when zey is seeing me, zey am running back up!"

Steven frowned. His sisters were here? And where was Madame Renault?

His heart thudding, Steven turned to Madame du Noir. "You wait for the next elevator," he said, looking at the long line. "Just try to get up to the top as soon as you can."

"And you?" Madame du Noir asked. "What will you do?"

Steven was already running. "I'm taking the stairs!" he cried over his shoulder. And as he darted up the first flight, he realized he didn't even care about being a hero.

All he cared about was saving his sisters' lives!

"Do you have any of the policeman's money left?" Elizabeth asked.

Jessica fished a couple of coins out of her pocket. "Why?" she asked curiously. They were back on top of the Eiffel Tower in the gathering twilight. Jessica's body ached all over from the long climb. She shivered in the cool air.

"There's a crowd down there at the bottom of the tower," Elizabeth said, reaching for one of the coin-operated telescopes. "I just want to see if Madame du Noir is down there, or—"

Jessica looked meaningfully at her sister, knowing how the sentence ended: *Or if she's on her way up here.* "I'll watch the elevator," she said, her mouth feeling like a block of wood. She was prepared to knock Madame du Noir out, too, if she had to.

"OK." Elizabeth dropped a coin into the slot and focused the telescope. "It's a long way down," she muttered, moving the eyepiece this way and that.

"Tell me about it," Jessica mumbled.

Jessica took up her post by the elevator. The platform was much less crowded than it had been, but pretty soon, a clump of tourists got off the elevator. She scanned their faces nervously. *Phew. No Madame du Noir.*

"Jess!" Elizabeth's voice sliced through the air.

Jessica looked up to see her sister motioning her furiously. "What's up?" she asked, rushing to Elizabeth's side.

"Look." Elizabeth thrust the telescope at Jessica.

Jessica had never seen such a happy expression on her twin's face. "What's up?" she asked curiously. She peered through the eyepiece.

"Is there anyone there that you recognize?" Elizabeth laid her hand on Jessica's shoulder.

Jessica glanced at her sister. "Seeing Madame du Noir through this thing is no reason to get excited, Elizabeth."

"Keep looking," Elizabeth urged her, jumping up and down on the balls of her feet.

Jessica sighed and looked again into the eyepiece. Suddenly an image leapt into view. She drew in her breath. "It's Mom," she said wonderingly.

She turned toward her sister. "It's—Mom!"

"Yes." Elizabeth blinked back tears. "Isn't it great?"

Jessica quickly turned back to the telescope. Sure enough, there was her mother, staring worriedly up toward the top of the tower. *Oh, Mom,* she thought, hardly able to hold back a grin.

"What do you think she's doing here?" Elizabeth asked.

"Who cares?" Jessica spun the telescope a little to the left. "And there's Dad next to her," she murmured. The telescope went blank as the time ran out, but Jessica didn't care. "Elizabeth!" she shouted, pumping her fists into the air. "We're saved!"

Madame du Noir gasped. At the front of the line, a very familiar-looking old woman was boarding the elevator.

"Madame Renault!" she muttered under her breath. Madame Renault looked like she was trying to blend in with a tour group, but Madame du Noir wasn't fooled for a minute. The pink-and-blue scarf was a dead giveaway.

Madame du Noir thought fast. Monsieur Courbet was nowhere to be seen—probably still trying to find a parking space—and Steven was running up the stairs after his sisters.

There was only one thing to be done.

"Pardon, pardon!" she murmured, pushing her way through the line and stepping into the elevator just as the doors began to close.

*   *   *

"We could go down the elevator," Elizabeth suggested.

"Are you kidding?" Jessica asked. "What if Madame du Noir is still down there, waiting with her big sheet of glass to smush us with?"

Elizabeth bit her lip. "OK. Tell you what. Another elevator's coming up." She nodded to the indicator. "Tell you what. If she's there, we'll run down the stairs."

"All right," Jessica said. "And if—and if she isn't there?"

"Then—" Elizabeth frowned. "Then we should go down the elevator. If we see her at the bottom, we can always push the button that closes the door and yell for help or something. OK?"

"OK." The girls took up a position halfway between the stairs and the elevator. Jessica held her breath and waited for the elevator doors to open.

Madame du Noir elbowed her way onto the front of the elevator just before the doors hissed shut. She had always hated elevators. They made her stomach hurt, and they were crowded. But right now, she had to admit, the crowd was a good thing.

Madame Renault was staring straight at the wall in front of her. She hadn't seen Madame du Noir yet. Or if she had, she hadn't recognized her.

"Pardon, pardon." Madame du Noir carefully pushed her way to the back of the elevator, just in case. A woman wearing a backpack frowned at her.

"My granddaughters," Madame du Noir said quickly in French. "I must get to my granddaughters."

The other woman sniffed and moved aside. Madame Renault was still looking at the wall.

Madame du Noir stared hard at Madame Renault for a moment. Something was odd—what was it?

She frowned. Then the truth hit her. Madame Renault's gray hair seemed to have grown on one side during the last few minutes, and shrunk on the other—as though she were wearing a wig.

When he had started running up the stairs, Steven had taken the steps three at a time. By the end of the second flight he was down to two at a time, and by now he was barely running at all. Sweat dripped off his forehead. *I've got to save them,* he thought anxiously, wiping his hair out of his eyes and chugging onward. He imagined Madame Renault honing in on his sisters, getting closer and closer. *I've got to—*

Steven clutched at his leg. "Cramps!" he moaned. *Doggone it, I should never have tried to run up these stairs.*

He wiggled his leg. Little explosions of pain shot through his body. Steven stared gloomily at the steps stretching ahead, farther and farther up.

And as he looked, his image of Madame Renault came into sharper and sharper focus. She had a gun—or maybe a knife. A large butcher's knife.

Steven's heart felt like a stone in his chest. Once more he took the steps. Pain or no pain, he didn't have any other choice.

*   *   *

The elevator door slowly slid open. Elizabeth clutched her sister's arm. "Remember, if she's on it, run," she hissed to Jessica. Jessica nodded, her eyes wide.

Passengers began pouring off the elevator. A *tour group*, Elizabeth thought. Several young women got off the elevator, talking and laughing.

The sight of the woman behind them made Elizabeth gasp.

"Jess!" she burst out, running forward. "It's her! Madame Renault!" Elizabeth yelled, waving her arms as the old lady stepped out onto the platform.

Madame Renault swung around. "You'll protect us, won't you?" she begged, coming closer to the old woman.

"Ah, yes, *mais oui*." Madame Renault's eyes glittered. "I protect you." With a strong, swift motion, she seized Jessica and Elizabeth by the wrists and pulled them over to the telescope area.

"Did you bring our bags?" Elizabeth asked hopefully, noticing that Madame Renault's mustache had somehow gotten thicker.

"No." Madame Renault pulled them even faster, so fast that Elizabeth struggled to keep her feet on the ground.

"Could you—umm—could you maybe pull a little more gently?" Jessica asked. Madame Renault grasped the girls even harder.

"Ay-lee-sa-bess!" A familiar voice echoed across the platform. Elizabeth turned around. Her heart began to thump in her chest.

Black-and-white scarf fluttering in the breeze,

Madame du Noir lurched toward them. Elizabeth thought she could see a crazed, frantic look in her eye.

"Don't kill us!" Jessica pleaded to Madame du Noir.

Madame Renault gripped Elizabeth's wrist even more firmly as Madame du Noir came closer. "Girls! Come wiss me!" Madame du Noir shouted. "I no kill you!"

"Zhessica!"

"Yeah, right!" Jessica burst out. "Madame Renault, you have to help us!"

With a sudden motion, Madame Renault dropped Elizabeth's arm and reached into her purse. Feeling suddenly unprotected, Elizabeth shrank back behind Madame Renault, just as the old woman pulled a long shiny knife. Elizabeth's eyes widened. *What on earth?* Then she felt a wave of relief. *Of course—to protect us. Now we'll be safe.*

"No!" With a shriek, Madame du Noir dashed toward Madame Renault, brandishing her own purse like a tennis racket. Elizabeth watched in horror as the handbag came down, thumping heavily on Madame Renault's head. Groaning, Madame Renault dropped the knife and sank—first to her knees, then to the ground.

"You've killed her!" Jessica stared at Madame du Noir.

Her head whirring, Elizabeth bent down over Madame Renault. *She's got to be all right,* she thought. *She's just got to!* But as she checked to see if the old lady was breathing, she noticed something peculiar.

"Her hair—" Elizabeth's words caught in her throat. "Jessica, her hair!" Forgetting Madame du Noir, Elizabeth stared down at Madame Renault. Madame Renault's beautifully styled shoulder-length gray hair was—

Elizabeth gulped.

Was lying beside her!

"When Madame du Noir hit Madame Renault with her handbag, she knocked off her hair," Elizabeth said slowly. "Which means it was only a wig. Which means—"

She stared at Madame Renault once more. She had a carefully trimmed brown crew cut, the same hairstyle Elizabeth had seen hundreds of men wearing around Sweet Valley.

Elizabeth clapped her hand over her mouth.

"She's really a man."

Jessica stared. "I guess that explains her mustache."

"Your friend Madame Renault is real-ly *Monsieur* Renault," Madame du Noir said grimly. "A good disguise for killer of young American girls, yes?"

"Madame—I mean, Monsieur Renault is the murderer?" Jessica whispered hoarsely.

Elizabeth felt dizzy. She glanced at the blue and pink scarf around "Madame" Renault's neck. "But I don't understand," she said, her breath coming in gasps. "The picture of the woman who was killing American tourists? She was wearing a black-and-white scarf—just like Madame du Noir."

Jessica nodded numbly. "Madame Renault's is

different. I mean, Monsieur Renault's. I mean—I don't know what I mean."

A blue scarf. Elizabeth strained to think. Madame du Noir's black-and-white scarf seemed to float in the breeze. "Of course! We saw a black-and-white photo," Elizabeth went on, her head beginning to clear. "A blue scarf would look black on black-and-white film. And light pink polka-dots—"

"Would look white," Jessica finished flatly.

They looked at each other. Slowly they stood up and faced Madame du Noir.

"Oops," Elizabeth mumbled.

It was all she could say.

Seventeen

"I am so, so, so, so sorry," Jessica groaned a few minutes later. She and Elizabeth had helped Madame du Noir tie up "Madame" Renault, using the two scarves. Then they had all carried the unconscious man to the waiting elevator while several tourists looked on curiously. "Madame du Noir, I promise that I will clean your kitchen floor every single day for the rest of my entire life."

"Me too. At least, every day that we stay with you." Elizabeth looked at Madame pleadingly, begging her forgiveness. *What do you say to a person who you thought was trying to kill you—when you find out she was actually trying to save you from a murderer?* she wondered. In fact, far from being a murderer, Madame du Noir actually seemed pretty neat.

"I tell you story, yes?" Madame du Noir asked.

"Yes," Elizabeth agreed, feeling a little relieved.

"I am remember when I am in school, age four,

age five," Madame du Noir began, a twinkle in her eye. The elevator picked up speed. "My mother is always pick up me, yes? But on zis day she cannot come at last moment. You see?"

Elizabeth nodded. "How did you get home?" she asked.

"Ah." The old woman grinned, and Elizabeth couldn't help grinning back. "My mother call ze school. 'My little daugh-tair, she will be pick up by my sis-tair, Sophie,' she tell zem. And zey tell me." She shrugged.

"So you were going to be picked up by your aunt," Jessica said slowly. On the floor, their little package moaned.

"Yes, yes, zat is right," Madame du Noir said. "Now come ze strange part, yes? I am see my aunt Sophie every day. I know her like I know"—she hesitated—"like I know ze hand of my own back."

"The back of my own hand," Elizabeth corrected her.

"Of course." Madame du Noir waved her arms. "But I am only four, pair-haps five, and I am sudden not remember zis. And so, I get picture in my brain." She tapped her head wisely. "Picture is not my aunt Sophie. It is a watch."

"A watch?" Elizabeth stared curiously at Madame du Noir.

"A watch," Madame du Noir repeated. "You know. Broomstick. Ugly. Black cats and magic and bumps on ze nose?"

"Oh, a *witch*," Elizabeth said, nodding. "You thought she was a witch."

"A witch, yes, yes." Madame du Noir's head bobbed up and down emphatically. "I am think my aunt Sophie are a witch, and I am cry, cry, cry, and nobody is knowing why. But zen at last I am see her—and I am remember ze truth." She grinned happily at Elizabeth and shrugged. "I am not look before I am leap."

Jessica giggled. "You should always look before you am leap. I mean—"

"I guess we just let our imaginations run away with us," Elizabeth added. She smiled at Madame du Noir.

Jessica smiled, too. "Yeah, you're not scary at all!"

Elizabeth nodded. "The idea that you could ever kill anybody!"

"Really," Jessica added as the elevator came to a stop. "I can't imagine anybody thinking such a crazy idea as that!"

"There they are!"

Mrs. Wakefield pointed to the elevator door and grabbed her husband's arm. Elizabeth and Jessica stepped off, looking much messier than she'd seen them in years. Dashing forward, Mrs. Wakefield seized the two girls in a huge embrace.

"Madame du Noir!" Mr. Wakefield exclaimed with surprise as he rushed toward his daughters. "What are you doing here? And what in the world is—" He reached out with his foot and poked the tied-up man on the floor of the elevator.

"Zis is ze killer." Monsieur Courbet stepped forward.

"The killer?" The blood drained out of Mrs. Wakefield's face.

"We tell you later," Monsieur Courbet added quickly. "For now, pair-haps you would like some of ze pastries you, ah——" He looked at the girls significantly. "Ze pastries you *help* me bake."

"Certainly," Mrs. Wakefield said, catching up the girls once more into a hug. "Anything. I'm so glad we're a family again," she mumbled. "But——"

"What?" Mr. Wakefield asked, his arms around his daughters.

Mrs. Wakefield stepped back and looked around. "Where's Steven?"

There can't be many more steps to go, Steven thought, gritting his teeth against the pain. He knew the best thing to do for leg cramps was to just stop moving, but he couldn't do that. Not with Madame Renault so close to his sisters. No way!

He turned a corner. The top of the staircase was in sight. *Phew,* he thought, inching up to the next stair. *Oh, boy, it hurts!* He thought back to the announcement he'd heard a few minutes back. It sounded like they were saying something about closing down the tower.

Stumbling up to the last landing, he flung open the door—and saw only darkness. "It's empty," he told himself, scanning the platform as the door banged shut behind him. "Jessica? Elizabeth?" he called, raising his voice and massaging his sore leg. "Where are you?"

There was no answer. Steven slumped down

onto the floor. "Great," he muttered. "All that work for nothing! They're gone."

He only wished he knew where.

"You did what?" Mr. Wakefield looked in surprise from Jessica back to the very woozy-looking policeman in front of him.

"Oh, Dad," Jessica murmured. She wished the police officer would just go away. With embarrassment she remembered how she had flung the door in his face. *I hope it didn't hurt him too much,* she thought. She faced the officer. "You see," she began, swallowing hard, "we thought a crazy old woman was after us, and it turned out we were right, but it wasn't the right crazy old woman, and anyway, the crazy old woman turned out to be a crazy old man." She gave the policeman her most charming smile. "Well, anyway, do you have any questions so far?"

"Well, for crying out loud!"

Steven stared at the door to the stairwell. Somehow it had automatically locked behind him. *Guess I'll try the elevators,* he thought, limping across the platform.

He jabbed his finger at the down button, but it refused to light up. In desperation he tried the up button as well. No luck.

"Figures," he mumbled. *My sisters get into the stupidest situations—and it's always up to me to get them out again.* He began to pace around the observation deck. *Somehow they always wind up golden. And it's me that gets the shaft!*

Elizabeth and Jessica were OK by now, he could feel it in his bones. But as for himself—

Steven sighed, a sense of worry rising in his stomach. "Is someone going to get me off this building?" he shouted off into space. He listened for an answer, but none came. *Of course not, Wakefield, you idiot,* he chided himself. *Who's going to hear you?*

Shaking his head, he took a deep breath. "They've gone away and closed this place down," he muttered miserably, staring across at the bright lights of Paris.

"And they've left me behind."

The policeman laughed gently after Jessica finished her explanation. "I will be all right," he told Jessica. "And now I understand what made you do it. But—" He wagged his forefinger at the twins. "Next time, you must look before you leap. I believe zat is ze right expression?"

"Umm . . . yeah," Jessica said humbly. She breathed a sigh of relief. *It's over,* she told herself. *Madame Renault—or should I say Monsieur Renault— has been taken off to jail, and Mom and Dad are here, and Madame du Noir is really nice, and Monsieur Courbet's pastries are absolutely delicious, even if we did drive him crazy, and tonight we can sleep in a real bed and have a hot shower.*

"I just wish we knew what happened to Steven," Mr. Wakefield said irritably as the group stepped out onto the sidewalk.

"Oh, he'll turn up," Jessica waved her hand dismissively. "I mean, we can't even lose him when we try, right, Lizzie?"

"Jessica!" Mrs. Wakefield said sternly.

"What is that?" One of the police officers raised a pair of binoculars to his eyes.

Curious, Jessica followed the direction he was aiming them. Her gaze traveled up to the top of the tower. She caught Elizabeth's sleeve. "Someone's up there," she said with surprise.

"Up where?" Elizabeth stared. Jessica pointed. There was a dim outline of a figure on the observation platform.

"A young man!" one of the policemen exclaimed. "I wonder who it can be."

Jessica shook her head slowly, suppressing a giggle.

She had a pretty good idea, all right!

Eighteen

"But wasn't the whole thing just plain hilarious?" Jessica asked, nibbling on her second croissant and staring anxiously at her parents.

Mr. and Mrs. Wakefield looked back at her sternly. "Hilarious," Mr. Wakefield repeated, folding his arms. "I don't think that's the word I would use."

It was early the next morning, and all the Wakefields were gathered around a table in Monsieur Courbet's bakery. Jessica felt refreshed after a good night's sleep. She and Elizabeth had had a good laugh listening to Steven's adventures trying to track them down and their father's difficulty in getting off the traffic circle with the rental car last night. She shook her head. If only her parents could lighten up a little, everything would be absolutely perfect.

Steven slumped against the table and groaned.

"My leg will probably never be the same again."

"We're sorry," Jessica told him, biting her lip to keep from laughing.

"Yeah, we're really—" Elizabeth dissolved into laughter.

Steven frowned. "Funny, but you don't *look* all that sorry!"

"I'm really sorry, Steven," Elizabeth gasped. "It's just the idea of you limping up those stairs—" She took a deep breath.

Jessica began to giggle, too. "While we were safely down at the bottom already!"

"Try to be a hero, and this is the thanks I get," Steven grumbled, wolfing down a pastry. "See if I ever try to rescue you again."

Mrs. Wakefield sighed. "I just wish you two had thought for a minute," she said. "Didn't it ever occur to you—even once—that the *Bonjour, Paris!* people wouldn't send you to live with a murderer?"

Jessica tried not to catch Elizabeth's eye. "Once or twice," she admitted. "But things kept happening."

"It all seemed to fit together so well," Elizabeth agreed, wiping the tears out of her eyes. "We kept overhearing things, and we just kept misunderstanding."

"Like when Madame du Noir told Monsieur Courbet that she was *with* our mother, and Elizabeth thought she said she *was* our mother," Jessica added, sneaking a quick look at her sister.

Elizabeth turned pink. "Or when Madame du

Noir said, 'I'll cook them and put them under glass,' and Jessica thought she meant us."

"Well, so did you," Jessica pointed out.

Elizabeth began to giggle again. "And it turned out that she was talking about some fancy way of cooking chicken. To welcome us on our first day in Paris!"

"Get it?" Jessica slapped her thigh. "She meant, 'I'll cook the pieces of chicken and put them—'"

"I get it, I get it!" Steven snarled.

Monsieur Courbet came into the room and tripped over a chair. "A funny story, yes?" he asked the Wakefields as he straightened up. "I am laugh all night long. Here is ze twins, running from a safe woman into ze arms of a murderer. Ha ha!" He laughed delightedly. "Ah, youth! Funny, no?"

"No," Steven said sourly.

"It was a good thing Madame du Noir swung her handbag when she did," Elizabeth said. "We thought Madame Renault was going to attack her, but I guess she was planning to go for us instead."

Jessica nodded. Even though the scene on the Eiffel Tower was only yesterday, it felt as if it had been ages ago. "Can you believe it? Here we were in Madame Renault's apartment, and we never caught on that she was really a man. Isn't that outrageous?"

Mr. and Mrs. Wakefield looked at each other and sighed.

"A riot," Monsieur Courbet agreed. His eyes danced. "Ah, youth!"

*   *   *

The door of the bakery opened a few minutes later. Elizabeth started as a familiar figure came in—an old woman in a black dress and a black-and-white polka-dotted scarf.

But Madame du Noir is our friend now, she reminded herself with a little laugh. She shook her head. It was hard to get rid of old feelings completely!

"I have news!" Madame du Noir cried out, waving an envelope over her head. "A telegram from ze Monteclaires!"

"The who?" Jessica whispered to Elizabeth.

"Don't you remember?" Elizabeth asked. "The family that was going to host us at first. Remember?" She gave her sister a nudge with her elbow. "Alain Monteclaire and his really cool car?"

"Oh, right!" Jessica exclaimed, her eyes lighting up.

Elizabeth turned back to Madame du Noir. "What does it say?"

"I will translate," Madame du Noir sat down next to Steven. She unfolded the letter. "Zey say grandmama is much better. And zey would like—" Raising her eyebrows, she smiled at Steven. "Oh, zey are out of zeir minds. Zey would like you to come stay wiss zem in Nice for ze rest of your trip."

"They what?" Steven wrinkled his face and stuck his tongue out.

"To Nice!" Elizabeth jumped out of her chair.

"We're going to Nice!" Jessica shouted at the same moment.

"Ah, youth," Monsieur Courbet said happily.

"I bet there'll be tons of really cute guys," Jessica said excitedly. "I mean, a ton of 'beaux garçons.' She smiled at her parents. "That's 'cute guys' in French."

"And probably not any lunatics," Elizabeth added. "Besides us, I mean."

Mr. Wakefield cleared his throat. "Well, girls, I'm afraid I have bad news for you." He looked meaningfully at his wife.

"Yes," Mrs. Wakefield piped in. "It seems to me, you've already had a pretty full vacation. Let's see. Sleeping in Napoléon III's bed at the Louvre, knocking a policeman out cold at the Eiffel Tower—"

"Making friends with a crazy killer in disguise," Mr. Wakefield added.

"France has had enough of the Wakefields," Mrs. Wakefield said firmly. "We leave Paris tomorrow morning."

"We do?" Elizabeth asked blankly.

"Mom!" Jessica wailed.

"Tomorrow morning," Mr. Wakefield repeated, frowning. "Figure out what you'd like to do today, because, girls, this is it."

Elizabeth wrinkled her nose. For a moment, she thought back to her time in Paris. She had to admit, her parents had a point.

"But what will we do for the rest of our spring break?" Jessica moaned.

"Oh, there's plenty to do." Mrs. Wakefield laughed. "There's my new garden and there's cleaning out the attic, for starters."

Jessica grimaced. "Sorry I asked."

"Ne-vair mind," Madame du Noir said comfortingly. "Some other time you come back to Paris. When you are a little older. And you stay wiss me zen. We have fun." She poked Jessica. "We not go to any art museums, yes?"

Jessica couldn't help but smile. She turned to her sister. "So what are we going to do today, then, Lizzie?"

Elizabeth smiled. "You have to ask?" she said. Seizing her twin's hand, she stood up.

"Let's do *le shopping!*" the girls cried at the same moment.

Bantam Books in the SWEET VALLEY TWINS series.
Ask your bookseller for the books you have missed.

SIGN UP FOR THE SWEET VALLEY HIGH® FAN CLUB!

Hey, girls! Get all the gossip on Sweet Valley High's® most popular teenagers when you join our fantastic Fan Club! As a member, you'll get all of this really cool stuff:

- Membership Card with your own personal Fan Club ID number
- A Sweet Valley High® Secret Treasure Box
- Sweet Valley High® Stationery
- Official Fan Club Pencil (for secret note writing!)
- Three Bookmarks
- A "Members Only" Door Hanger
- Two Skeins of J. & P. Coats® Embroidery Floss with flower barrette instruction leaflet
- Two editions of *The Oracle* newsletter
- Plus exclusive Sweet Valley High® product offers, special savings, contests, and much more!

Be the first to find out what Jessica & Elizabeth Wakefield are up to by joining the Sweet Valley High® Fan Club for the one-year membership fee of only $6.25 each for U.S. residents, $8.25 for Canadian residents (U.S. currency). Includes shipping & handling.

Send a check or money order (do not send cash) made payable to "Sweet Valley High® Fan Club" along with this form to:

SWEET VALLEY HIGH® FAN CLUB, BOX 3919-B, SCHAUMBURG, IL 60168-3919

NAME _____

(Please print clearly)

ADDRESS _____

CITY _____ STATE _____ ZIP _____

AGE _____ BIRTHDAY ____ / ____ / ____

(Required)

©1993 by Francine Pascal

Offer good while supplies last. Allow 6-8 weeks after check clearance for delivery. Addresses without ZIP codes cannot be honored. Offer good in USA & Canada only. Void where prohibited by law.

LCI-1383-193

A BANTAM SKYLARK BOOK

FRANCINE PASCAL'S

SWEET VALLEY TWINS AND FRIENDS.®

☐	BEST FRIENDS #1		1555-1/$3.25
☐	TEACHER'S PET #2		15656-X/$3.25
☐	THE HAUNTED HOUSE #3		15657-8/$3.25
☐	CHOOSING SIDES #4		15658-6/$3.25
☐	SNEAKING OUT #5		15659-4/$3.25
☐	THE NEW GIRL #6		15660-8/$3.25
☐	THREE'S A CROWD #7		15661-6/$3.25
☐	FIRST PLACE #8		15662-4/$3.25
☐	AGAINST THE RULES #9		15676-4/$3.25
☐	ONE OF THE GANG #10		15677-2/$3.25
☐	BURIED TREASURE #11		15692-6/$3.25
☐	KEEPING SECRETS #12		15702-7/$3.25
☐	STRETCHING THE TRUTH #13		15654-3/$3.25
☐	TUG OF WAR #14		15663-2/$3.25
☐	THE OLDER BOY #15		15664-0/$3.25
☐	SECOND BEST #16		15665-9/$3.25
☐	BOYS AGAINST GIRLS #17		15666-7/$3.25
☐	CENTER OF ATTENTION #18		15668-3/$3.25
☐	THE BULLY #19		15667-5/$3.25
☐	PLAYING HOOKY #20		15606-3/$3.25
☐	LEFT BEHIND #21		15609-8/$3.25
☐	OUT OF PLACE #22		15628-4/$3.25
☐	CLAIM TO FAME #23		15624-1/$2.75
☐	JUMPING TO CONCLUSIONS #24		15635-7/$2.75
☐	STANDING OUT #25		15653-5/$3.25
☐	TAKING CHARGE #26		15669-1/$3.25

Buy them at your local bookstore or use this handy page for ordering:

Bantam Books, Dept. SVT3, 2451 S. Wolf Road, Des Plaines, IL. 60018

Please send me the items I have checked above. I am enclosing $_____
(please add $2.50 to cover postage and handling). Send check or money
order, no cash or C.O.D.s please.

Mr/Ms _____

Address _____

City/State _____ Zip _____

Please allow four to six weeks for delivery.
Prices and availability subject to change without notice.

SVT3-1/94

SWEET VALLEY KIDS

Jessica and Elizabeth have had lots of adventures in *Sweet Valley High* and *Sweet Valley Twins*...now read about the twins at age seven! You'll love all the fun that comes with being seven—birthday parties, playing dress-up, class projects, putting on puppet shows and plays, losing a tooth, setting up lemonade stands, caring for animals and much more! It's all part of SWEET VALLEY KIDS. Read them all!

☐	JESSICA AND THE SPELLING-BEE SURPRISE #21	15917-8	$2.99
☐	SWEET VALLEY SLUMBER PARTY #22	15934-8	$2.99
☐	LILA'S HAUNTED HOUSE PARTY #23	15919-4	$2.99
☐	COUSIN KELLY'S FAMILY SECRET #24	15920-8	$2.99
☐	LEFT-OUT ELIZABETH #25	15921-6	$2.99
☐	JESSICA'S SNOBBY CLUB #26	15922-4	$2.99
☐	THE SWEET VALLEY CLEANUP TEAM #27	15923-2	$2.99
☐	ELIZABETH MEETS HER HERO #28	15924-0	$2.99
☐	ANDY AND THE ALIEN #29	15925-9	$2.99
☐	JESSICA'S UNBURIED TREASURE #30	15926-7	$2.99
☐	ELIZABETH AND JESSICA RUN AWAY #31	48004-9	$2.99
☐	LEFT BACK! #32	48005-7	$2.99
☐	CAROLINE'S HALLOWEEN SPELL #33	48006-5	$2.99
☐	THE BEST THANKSGIVING EVER #34	48007-3	$2.99
☐	ELIZABETH'S BROKEN ARM #35	48009-X	$2.99
☐	ELIZABETH'S VIDEO FEVER #36	48010-3	$2.99
☐	THE BIG RACE #37	48011-1	$2.99
☐	GOODBYE, EVA? #38	48012-X	$2.99
☐	ELLEN IS HOME ALONE #39	48013-8	$2.99
☐	ROBIN IN THE MIDDLE #40	48014-6	$2.99
☐	THE MISSING TEA SET #41	48015-4	$2.99
☐	JESSICA'S MONSTER NIGHTMARE #42	48008-1	$2.99
☐	JESSICA GETS SPOOKED #43	48094-4	$2.99
☐	THE TWINS BIG POW-WOW #44	48098-7	$2.99
☐	ELIZABETH'S PIANO LESSONS #45	48102-9	$2.99

Bantam Books, Dept. SVK2, 2451 S. Wolf Road, Des Plaines, IL 60018

Please send me the items I have checked above. I am enclosing $_____ (please add $2.50 to cover postage and handling). Send check or money order, no cash or C.O.D.s please.

Mr/Ms _____

Address _____

City/State _____ Zip _____

Please allow four to six weeks for delivery.
Prices and availability subject to change without notice.

SVK2-1/94